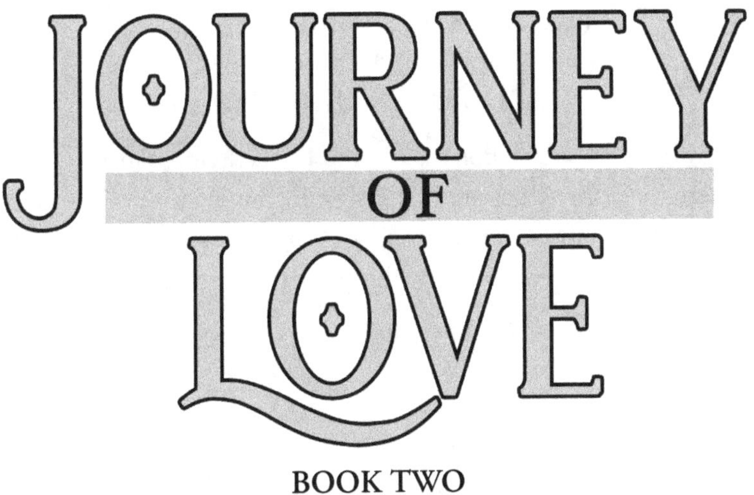

JOURNEY OF LOVE

BOOK TWO

Looking for Love in the Land of
Dharma, Karma and Chicken Masala

FRED ALAN ROBBINS

To my family and friends
The adventure continues.

Thank you for reading pages
Finding lost commas
and putting quotation marks
Where they belong

AND

To my guru and friend
Master Ketut Arsana
For his constant support
Love and friendship

*"The source of a true smile
Is an awakened mind."*

— Thich Nhat Hanh,
from *Peace is Every Step*

*"If you fear the snake
The snake will come."*
— Master Ketut Arsana

Max and Lea

It was a beautiful day in Ubud. The sun was playing hide and seek with the clouds, and there was a welcome ocean breeze coming in from the East. Max tugged at his backpack, but before putting it over his shoulders and riding off on his scooter for a joy ride, he sat down on the cement bench in front of the Ganesha sculpture. Whenever he sat there, he knew he was taking a chance on a rollercoaster ride of emotions, but that would be part of the experience. Ganesha, the remover of obstacles, was sometimes not up to the task for these moments. Memories would come rushing to the front of his mind instead of staying way in the back in a safer place where he could call upon them if he was feeling nostalgic.

It was almost two years since Dori's passing, and life as it was with Dori morphed quite easily into the life he now had with Lea. He knew that had more to do with her non-judgmental and mindful take on life than anything he contributed. It also didn't escape him at times like these, that he had an unhealthy habit of being overly hard on himself. He knew he held back even in their most passionate moments. Not because he wanted to, but because just like with Dori, there were too many times he felt more comfortable keeping his thoughts to himself. *When will this ever change?* he wondered. He knew only he could answer this question. He also knew he was still afraid to say it out loud and face it.

Max and Lea quickly settled into a happy life. They lived in the same villa he and Dori lived in, and in spite of the impossible to escape memories and energies, they found a harmony in sharing many of the common interests that brought them together in the first place. They allowed each other to feel free and independent of one another as needed. There was no jealousy, possessiveness, or any other relationship issues that generally come up if you are with someone long enough. At least, that's what they each thought to themselves. Max more-so than Lea as it turned out.

He was no longer seeing images of hearts traced on foggy windows left by his angel, Dori. His life with Lea was a fulfilling one. They shared the deep intimacy of a true friendship. They had passion, but it came from a different place than what he had with Dori. Dori was love mixed with lust. It revived them each in a different way, and came after years of unexpected celibacy. With Lea, the sex was more gentle. It was tender and caring with an occasional moment of abandon. It was good. It was comfortable. It was also not to be forever.

Max had learned enough about forevers in his lifetime, and though he promised to stay within himself, keep to being present and in the moment, and grateful for all that he had been blessed to receive, there were still times he forgot lessons learned. Just ask his mentor, Guru Ketut.

He became careless, and too many times took for granted the sweet, unconditional love Lea had brought into his life. She couldn't help but notice, and words and actions that went mostly ignored for so many months, now took on a different meaning. Her perception became reality, either willed or on its own. Questions, suspicion and doubt where there never was any, creeped into their day to day life like hungry termites chewing through an abandoned building. It wouldn't be long before it all disintegrated like so much dust.

CHAPTER ONE

The Undoing

It was an idyllic night. The moon was just a tiny bit smaller than the full moon of the night before. It offered the perfect ambiance for romance. The parchment colored fabric decorating the windows was the ideal filter creating a mix of shadows and magic for an evening of endless possibilities. A gentle breeze drifted in through the open French Doors bringing with it a splash of cool air and the sweet aroma of the ocean. It was just the kind of night Max and Lea thought about when they included as much of nature as possible in creating their lair.

Max wanted Lea to be free from the occasionally heavy presence of Dori that could still be felt. He and Dori had a passionate love affair that started at Om Ham and ended in their villa with her illness taking her life just as they were getting started. None of us mere mortals can figure these things out, but with the help of his friends and the Guru at Om Ham, Max let go and did his best to make it clear to Lea this was her home now.

He told her the bedroom was hers to design and shape as she wanted. That was a good thing. Lea was an artist as much as she was a romantic, often told she was born in the wrong era. She placed scented candles on night stands, dressers, and the book shelves above their custom bamboo bed and mattress. Her touch was everywhere and it showed. From the hand-crafted quilts to the fluffy pillows, the mood was set. It was a night to make love, laugh and enjoy each other.

Lea was already naked under the percale sheets, lying on her left side, with her right hand on her right thigh. She waited for Max to join her. She already decided to put aside any of the insecurities that had been creeping into her mind lately about the state of her life with Max. He was a dreamer. She was a realist. She knew from the start, there was an expiration date on their partnership. She just had no idea when that date would materialize or how it would come to be. But nothing hindered their friendship. That was the saving grace. Maybe a night of passion would get things back to where they were when they first moved in together.

When he walked out of the bathroom towards her, she could see the residual steam from the shower clinging to his body. A slight aroma from the sandalwood incense came with him. She opened the sheets exposing her beautiful naked body. She was a vision of a Renaissance painting come to life. Her alabaster cheeks flushed with warmth in perfect contrast to her auburn hair. It was her silent invitation to a night of passion, lust and desires.

When Max reached the bed, he quickly slid in next to her lying on his back looking up, not at her. In that moment, Lea's mind raced again with questions. He usually took his time devouring her body with his eyes before he got under the covers with her. He often commented on her breasts, saying how beautiful they were and how much he loved looking at her naked in the moonlight.

Why is he being so quiet? she wondered. "Max," she whispered softly. His head tilted to her eyes. "Max," she said again, "are you okay?"

"Lea. Shit. I'm sorry. I got lost in there. That pulsating option felt so good on my shoulder, I didn't want it to stop. Remind me never to close my eyes in the shower again." He turned on his side towards her so that their bodies touched.

"I guess you did. Is that all? You were in there a long time."

"I know. I'm good. Seriously. Lea, right?" She couldn't help but laugh a little. He could be funny and aloof at the same time. Even when he was about to have sex. "You're gorgeous, you know." He moved closer, their knees and thighs touched.

Once their bodies touched, she threw the sheet over to the side of the bed. She let her right hand drift slowly down his chest twirling the occasional grey hair in her path. She kissed his lips gently, while her fingers teased their way lower between his legs. He returned her kisses, and massaged her breasts. It felt good. She was turned on, glad she didn't let her earlier thoughts keep her from a sweet, sexy night.

She felt him grow in her hands, then rolled over to straddle him. He moved underneath her with a moan of appreciation. Her fingers knew where to touch him. They had done this dance before. She circled lightly, her fingers mimicking a feather duster tracing top to bottom. She was a woman ready to fuck. She wanted him inside her. She wrapped a hand around his shaft to hold him so she could lower herself down onto him. She moved slowly, until they were sex to sex. Their bodies moved in sync, Max thrusting up, Lea pushing down. They played until passion took its toll and their eyes rolled happily closed, body to body.

Max's comfort was fleeting. It was 4 a.m. and he was awake sitting against the headboard writing in his bedside journal. Lea felt the tussle of the sheets enough to turn towards him with half open eyes. This was nothing new, so she let it go and fell back to sleep.

Moonlight was still the only light in the bedroom, but it was enough for him to write down his thoughts. He sat quietly against the headboard next to her, his legs against hers. Thankfully, she quickly fell back to sleep, half on her side, half on her back. She slept peacefully, rested from their night of passion. He read over the note he had just written, wondering if he should rip it up, or leave it on the bed and escape before she woke. The energy that shifted in their bedroom made his decision for him. Lea's eyes opened.

"Max? What is it? Why are you up?" Her eyes saw the note in his hand. "What is that?"

"Just some thoughts. You know I like to write when I can't sleep."

"Why can't you sleep?" she asked. "I felt you being restless half the night." Her voice was merely a throaty whisper from her sleepy state of being.

"It's just thoughts," he repeated. "I didn't mean to wake you. Mostly, I was just watching you sleep. You're so beautiful."

"Lie back down," she said patting the mattress. "We'll talk in the morning. Okay?"

Max leaned forward to kiss her. "Sounds good. I'm so tired." He tossed the note to the floor on his side of the bed. He got back under the covers. His eyes closed, relieved. He quickly fell back into a deep sleep.

He had no idea how long he slept until he woke up and realized he was alone. The sun was already halfway up. Lea was gone. He reached down for the note he threw on the floor. It was gone as well. "Shit," he said out loud to himself. He looked in the bathroom garbage can, then the kitchen. Nothing. He wasn't sure if that was a good thing or not. He couldn't even remember all that he wrote, other than he was sure it would hurt Lea's feelings if not explained.

"Fuck!" he said out loud. *This is not good.* He dressed quickly, then filled his backpack with enough clothes for a few days of escape.

Later, he stood a bit uneasily next to his white Vespa scooter. He looked around, and then up at the sky as if looking for directions, then patted down his pockets from top to bottom. "Ahh," he mumbled. Then he smiled, shaking his head. He realized he left his phone on the bedroom nightstand. "Wallet, keys, phone, wallet, keys, phone," he repeated out loud. *How many times must I repeat this mantra before I finally leave the house without forgetting something?*

He left his backpack at the fountain and walked purposefully into his villa, leaving the front door open. He grabbed an apple and a banana from the ceramic fruit bowl on the kitchen counter, and went into his and Lea's bedroom. He saw his phone, grabbed it, and put it in his left front shirt pocket. He stopped for a moment to look around, as if a little more time would give him an answer.

He peered out the French doors that led to the yard. There was a clear view to the back deck and flower garden that Dori, and now Lea, loved working on. Lea planted lemon grass, turmeric and lots of flowers. She didn't want to erase Dori, but she wanted her own identity to be alive, seen and felt.

Lea called out as she walked through the open front door. She'd gotten up early to go into town for some fresh bagels and sweets. She'd read the note Max had written and subconsciously left on the floor for her to find. She understood by now that he liked to get away when he had questions. That was his way out instead of just dealing with things head on. It wasn't mean, but it still hurt. His note expressed his thoughts on being friends more than lovers and that he needed some time to make sense of things. She felt bad for him more than she was angry. "Honey, it's me. Where are you?"

Her voice was still hopeful. That was who she was. She wanted to leave the note in the past if it made sense. Maybe her worst fears were just that — fears. Fear is an illusion after all. Nothing like fresh rolls and hot coffee to begin a conversation and change things to a positive state of mind. She placed the pink bakery box on the kitchen counter.

"Hello?" she called again, more as a question than a greeting. As she walked further into their plant filled villa, her mind started to connect some familiar dots. She noticed Max's backpack at the base of the fountain next to his scooter. His helmet was already hanging on the handlebars. It was usually in the closet unless he was going somewhere.

To Max, she sounded like one of the many songbirds that graced their property like angels sent directly to help keep their spirits high. Her voice was happy and soothing. She was like the Balinese people in that she avoided confrontation if at all possible. He snapped out of his mini trance and walked out of their bedroom towards the kitchen.

"Are you going somewhere?" Lea asked as he came into her line of vision. The butterflies in her stomach were all the information she needed. She'd felt queasy talking to the empty space between them and it wasn't much better now that he was standing right in front of her.

"I don't know," he replied, knowing his cowardly escape had been thwarted.

"It kinda looks like you are," she said.

"I guess I am. I was about to leave a note. I'll text you later, okay? I need to get out of town for a day or two and the mountains feel right."

"That's all right, Max. I don't want a text and I don't need *another* note. I have the one you wrote last night. It's all pretty clear, don't you think?"

"Like I said last night, it was just thoughts. I can't really explain it right now."

"Let me help you." Lea's voice was going up, getting stronger as she felt her footing beneath her. "You've been so aloof lately. I've started to feel like a stranger in my own home. And you don't have a clue. I could've come home with blue hair and a nose ring, and you wouldn't have noticed."

"Lea...I'm so sorry. And I would've noticed a nose ring." That remark raised her eyebrows an inch. "I'm sorry. That was stupid. What can I do?"

"That's for you to figure out. All I know right now is that I'm not going to chance another night like last night when I put myself out there with my silly expectations only to have you tell me you're not sure we should be romantic."

"They are not silly expectations. You're beautiful and sweet and amazing and I'm really sorry. I loved last night up until the note part."

"You know what. I love you. And I know you love me. But we both know there is something going on that maybe neither of us wants to talk about or admit to. People change, feelings change, everything changes. I can't try to make this better, or create a romance that I know deep down is not what we have together. You said as much in your note."

Max's energy and posture shifted to pure defense. "That note is not all true. What I said about romance and friendship was just me talking to myself in writing. I do feel romantic with you, but I know you also deserve more. Way more."

"You're a good guy, Max. But my heart is telling me to be true to myself with what makes me happiest in a loving relationship. Maybe my happiest heart is one without you as my lover. Romance comes from the heart and there's no faking it. I don't want you to *try*."

Those words hit him hard. His stomach bounced up and down a few times. "You can't mean that. You couldn't possibly be here for all this time and not be happy. Could you?"

"You're not the only one who keeps feelings and emotions inside. Just go, Max. It will be good for both of us. I know the mountains are good for you, so…"

Lea stopped. She felt there was nothing more to say. There was still a knot in her stomach the size of a large avocado. For her, that was something to pay attention to. That was at least one thing they shared equally from all this.

Max also stopped. There was probably more he could say, but in the end, it would just be words that wouldn't make a difference. Instead of talking, he walked quietly past her, head down. He felt too small to look her in the eyes.

CHAPTER TWO

Back to Kintamani

Max felt at home in the mountains. It was July in Bali, one of the warmest months of the year, and the perfect time to enjoy the cooler air near the top of Mount Batur. The rainy season, which had been much harder and longer than usual, had finally passed. Climate change was alive and well even in his Bali paradise.

He wanted to try a new hotel, and eventually decided on Batur Mountain View. It was a small hotel, similar to the Black Lava Hostel where he met Fleur, but farther away from Kintamani and with a close-up view of the mountain. Both the small breakfast area and the yoga shala faced the mountain directly.

Maybe there would be an eruption. That would surely match my mental state and the condition of my emotional self. At least he had the fortitude and clarity to laugh about that. He remembered reading "laughter in the face of adversity was the sign of an elevated consciousness." He wondered who said it and if a meeting was possible.

Facing the majestic, supernatural mountain was all the inspiration he needed. He laid down the yoga mat he'd brought along, and in short order he was sitting cross-legged, doing his kundalini breathing techniques, or pranayama, as it is called in yoga circles.

The fast in-out breath work always lifted his spirits and his state of consciousness. It was the combination of strong exhalation while pulling your stomach inwards and at the same time, making the sound of a hissing snake. Sssst, Sssst, Sssst. The highlight of this pranayama was the squeezing of the anus, or root chakra, on each Sssst sound to lock in the kundalini energy and lift it from the lower chakras to the crown.

He pointed his arms straight out with his fingers interlocked and his two index fingers pointing forward. He was in a solid rhythm, moving from one hand position (mudra) to another. This technique, while very powerful, did not mean a person couldn't be distracted.

In his heightened state of mind, Max felt the slightest break from the sun's warm rays that were caressing his face. It was just a moment, but he could not help but look up. Standing a few feet to his left, he noticed the long shadow and slender frame of a tall woman with a straw sunhat on her head. Dark blonde hair trailed down past her neck and over her shoulders. She was wearing a white sleeveless dress with lace cutouts on the backside in the shape of a dream catcher — the kind often found on a bedroom door or hanging over the bed itself.

He stopped his breath work and was drawn into the detailed and spiritual ink depicting the god Ganesha that ran up and down her arms in brilliant blues and reds. Ganesha, the God with the face of an elephant, is the God of removing obstacles and enhancing personal protection, and is often found in the form of big sculptures in front of many of the hotels and villas that line the roads of Ubud, Bali.

There was also what appeared to be the face of a goddess that started at the base of her neck and went down past her shoulder blades. He wanted to see more. The faint hint in the see-through lace had him wondering what else was being hidden from view.

"I'm Satya," she said as she turned around. She'd noticed that he had shifted a bit from his breathing pose. "I didn't mean to disturb you."

"Not at all. I could hardly call this a disturbance. I'm Max," he replied. Max paused a moment. Then added, "Your Ganesha is beautiful."

"Thank you. It was done by a friend of mine in Uluwatu, and it's very special to me."

"I can see why. Your friend is an incredible artist."

"Thank you," Satya answered. "Do you mind if I sit down next to you?"

"Of course not." Max lifted off his yoga mat and turned it sideways so Satya could sit down next to him.

"I've heard and practiced that style of breathing before. Kundalini tantra, right? Have you been to India?"

"Not yet," Max replied. "I've thought about it, but it doesn't feel right for me. Even my guru looked at me when I asked about going and he said point blank, 'Max, India is not for you.' Do you want to join me for some breathing?" Max asked. "I was going to do a few more minutes before sundown."

"Not right now. That's not why I'm here."

Max wasn't sure what to make of that remark, but whatever her reason was, he felt a charge of electricity running through him. Certainly, she wasn't some narcissistic influencer only on top of the mountain for a selfie. That would surely ruin the moment. So, he looked up at Satya who was a few inches taller than him, and smiled.

She went on. "So tell me, Max, what frightens you about India?"

"I can't really be specific. I don't necessarily think of it as being frightened about anything. I just don't feel a need to go. Not everyone has to go to India as some sort of right of passage into the world of spirituality."

"Hmmm. That sounds angry or maybe envious. You can be specific if you want to be. You don't have to worry about offending me. India can be many different things to many different people. Just like Bali or any place else in the world. And we're not talking about everyone — only you."

"Well, my guru said I would be there ten minutes and—"

"I'm not asking what your guru said," Satya cut him off. "People have reasons for not wanting to do things. Let me ask again. What frightens you about India?"

Max fell into a momentary silence, thinking. *If I tell the truth if will I lose all chance of spending more time with this incredible, mysterious and exotic woman who appeared out of nowhere?* He knew nowhere was not a place. She'd appeared from *somewhere. Is she a guide? A way-shower as people from other dimensions who are here to help us when asked are called?* All these possibilities raced through his fully engaged mind. *What we perceive is often wrong.* He knew that, but it still often evaded him in real time, when it counted the most.

Satya moved closer, her long, tan legs barely touching his. He could feel the heat her energy emanating from her body through the thin fabric. *It's nice,* he thought, as he started to lose his focus on everything else. *She has no fear.*

She gently touched his shoulder and turned him more directly toward her, as her dark green eyes stared directly into his soft baby blues. "If you tell me what you are afraid of, you are one step closer to surrendering to it."

That sounded like a quote from a book of quotes on how to find your true self, or some other guide to spiritual enlightenment. *Who is this woman?* he asked himself again. *Is she some kind of mystic who arrived to save me from myself?* Max loved how fast his mind would choose the most far out of the ordinary explanation of events that he was often not able to be put into words. *People say there are as many mystics in India as there are shattered dreams walking down Hollywood Boulevard. Take that for a quote, lady,* he wanted to say out loud. He could speak to Hollywood, but India?

"I don't want to see people pissing and shitting in front of me as I walk down the street. It's so depressing and disgusting and revolting to me. Is that good enough?" Max's answer was harsh and he knew it the moment it came out. It angered him to have to answer and reveal something personal to a woman he'd just met. It didn't help that he also found her insanely attractive. It was hard to explain, but he felt more at ease opening up to someone he didn't feel attracted to. That was definitely an issue that needed attention.

"It's a start," Satya answered. She was kind in her answer without even the slightest hint of judgement.

Max judged it, though. He knew it was a bullshit excuse. He didn't like to see people suffering and living in squalor. It made him feel helpless. At home in California, he could at least give a few dollars and a smile to a person who was sitting with their hands out for help in front of a grocery store. He knew that helped make that one day a little better. *But what could I do when facing a hundred people lined up along the Ganges river bed all asking for help with their hands out begging for food or money? Or the countless women holding little babies sitting in front of Bali Buda on Hanoman street calling out "mister" "mister" as I walk by.* He thought if he avoided seeing it, it wasn't really there. Like the famous Bali dogs.

He wanted to take his scooter rides with blinders on to keep himself focused only on what was directly in front of him. And if he could have his complete choice in the matter, he would rather find his spiritual nirvana while at a clean, nicely located yoga retreat with Wi-Fi and great air conditioning than on a dusty road with snakes and insects and the fear of thinking each sip of water might be his last sip of anything. *Who knows? Seeing people from Nepal and Rishikesh at the Om Ham pool may be as close to India as I ever get.*

"People suffer all over the world, Max. In India, however, it's so close to you that you can't escape it. You can't pretend it doesn't exist, either. People travel from all over the world to find the source of their pain and let it go once and for all. You either want the answers or you don't," Satya said rather emphatically.

"Bali serves the same purpose for me. If you don't mind, I would like to get back to my breathing."

"Of course. We all have our karma."

"I understand. But that has nothing to do with how *I* feel. Do *you* understand?"

"More than you know. May I ask you one more question?"

The tension drained from Max's face and some of the color came back with it. "Sure."

"Tell me, what do you really gain if you continue to run and hide from the things that are uncomfortable for you? There is a reason for it and I believe it's important for you to find out what it is. I would like to help you if you let me."

He didn't answer. He turned his face slightly away, looking at the mountain for help.

Fuck!, he thought to himself. *Is she reading my mind?* As he was thinking of what else to say, his mind went to thoughts of his beloved dog Jake, who'd recently passed, and his parents who'd passed just before that, and on and on until tears fell slowly from his eyes and rolled down his cheeks.

Satya tapped Max's hand and then gripped it tightly, pulling him to her until he could feel her beating heart against his. He could feel the warmth and kindness inside her. "When your father was near the end, lying in his bed, pale with his life force slipping away with each breath, you never went into the bedroom to sit beside him. Do you want to understand why?"

He answered quickly without taking even a second to figure out how she could know that. "I know why. He didn't need me to. He knew I loved him."

"Not until near the very end, Max. The reason is because you didn't want to sit there and cry. You were afraid to reveal that incredible loving heart you try so hard to protect so you can appear strong. Instead of letting go, you fight against yourself to hold back the beautiful vulnerability that is your essence. That's where your real strength lies. Let it shine and watch your life change."

Satya wrapped her long arms around him, squeezing gently but firmly. She held him as the fire from within her passed into him. Then, as she merged into the mist, she whispered in his ear. "Don't be afraid of real love, Max. Bali can be your India."

CHAPTER THREE

Lucid Dreams

The cool mountain air and the setting sun brought Max back into the present moment. He looked left and right, but there was no sign of Satya. His hand still felt warm from her touch. He put it to his face to see if he could feel it there as well. He did. He gathered himself and went into his room to order some food and make sense of this unexpected experience, if he could.

He'd had lucid dreams before. He was just now learning about living in an awakened state — living in the 5th dimension as it is called. The 5th dimension is a state of love, a frequency of energy that makes one feel in a joyous state living without judgment and ego and right and wrong. How nice is that? Now that he knew what it was, he was able to put it in perspective and choose that over a more ego-filled life.

He'd even experienced astral travel as a young man of 28. It was still so alive in his mind that it was like it just happened the night before. He could recount the whole night. It started in the bedroom of his Chicago apartment with the sensation of lifting up out of his body and floating away from the bed. Well, the real start was the breath work and rapid kundalini breathing techniques designed to give the mind and third eye a little push toward a higher state of consciousness. He did that for thirty minutes before getting into bed.

He smiled as he remembered traveling above the streets of Chicago in his sleep. He passed over Wrigley Field, home of the Chicago Cubs baseball team. He watched Christmas shoppers in the famous downtown Marshal Fields Department store, and he flew over the Chicago El train tracks to the Howard Street stop. He remembered every minute of it.

Max enjoyed thinking about it because it made him happy when he experienced such spiritual and metaphysical moments. It also reinforced his belief that with a little effort a person can live on a higher plane of consciousness; not the plane of regular 3rd dimensional life where time and ego rule that world — an era of punching corporate time clocks, the ten-minute work break, and following mass media that was specifically designed to keep society in control.

Thank god, he thought, *I was never a time card puncher.* He'd never followed the crowds or the rules, much to his parents' dismay. Now some of his attitudes and behavior made more sense to him. He didn't know what to call it. Weird would work, which was why it wasn't something he would openly share until he felt he was in a safe enough space to talk about it. This was another reason he started Max Talks.

But this brush with higher dimension beings, guides like Satya, was new. It was entirely different from any experience he'd ever had.

There *was* one time that was eerily similar, during an earlier trip to Bali. It happened at the Yoga Barn in Ubud, at his regular Tuesday night Tibetan Bowl meditation group led by Wakuha. She was a well-known Balinese healer and teacher.

At the start of each session, as she sprinkled holy water from her well over the heads of all the students, she always reminded the class to set an intention for the meditation. This particular night, he'd asked for his cousin Brad, his best friend throughout all their years together from the age of five, to pay him a visit. Brad had passed away four years earlier, and for whatever reason, that was what had popped into his mind.

So, he asked for a brief visit. "Say hi, dear Brad. It's been too long." Sure enough, about twenty minutes into the meditation, he felt goosebumps on his arms, which he now knew was one of the signs of being in the 5th dimension. He woke up from his relaxed state to see his cousin's smiling face go buzzing past his eyes. Brad's wavy black hair led the way, followed by a big, wide smile showing his full set of pearly white teeth, which was funny because his last name was Pearl.

This lasted only seconds, but added to the proof he needed to understand that the universe was a happy and willing participant in our lives if we knew how and when to ask. The power of the mind and concentrating on manifesting desires can make anything happen. Amazing.

Before Max was completely dry from a much-needed long, hot shower, there was a knock on his door. A local food delivery service called Grab had brought his meal. He thanked the young man with a nice tip and sat down at his little patio table to enjoy a hot and aromatic dinner of shaksuka with poached eggs, a popular Middle Eastern dish served in Turkey and Israel and, he was happy to see, here in Bali.

The dish wasn't exactly as he had come to know it back home in California, but that was a good thing. This Indonesian version came with a choice of either duck or chicken eggs, tangy mung bean sauce, young jackfruit, avocado, crispy fried sourdough bread, and parsley salsa. *Time to dig in!* he thought with enthusiasm.

Tired and full, Max put on some Krisha Das mantra music and looked out his window at the bright glow of a new quarter moon sitting on top of the mountain. Soon, his mind went to the way he'd left things at home with Lea.

She deserves so much more from me. I left without any consideration of how she might have interpreted my actions. Even worse, I'm not quite sure how to fix it. He had a depressing thought. *Maybe I'm just too darn happy on my own to be much good to anyone else.*

He enjoyed the company of women and didn't mind going home alone after a long day or short night of friendly conversation and laughter. However, that didn't stop him from wanting someone to live with him and put up with his selfishness. At this rate, he knew he was piling on to his karmic debt at a pace that would prevent him from paying it off before he moved on and into the next cycle.

His sexual desires had most definitely been awakened in the past couple of years. Fleur… He smiled at the memory of her and the sweet, gentle erotic play they shared. She was the right angel at the right time. He wondered about her. They fit in all the ways that made sense for that time and that place. She got his jokes, she loved to tease him and play with his long graying hair, and she always wore a smile. They each felt it, but their personal directions in life took them on separate journeys.

We were able to smile from the heart and allow our time together to pass as one of those great moments in life to be appreciated for what it was without trying to make more out of it. Probably not a bad way to look at everything in life, attachments and expectations and all that, he thought to himself.

Physically, he was strong and his body was back to working on all cylinders. He no longer had to avoid the smiles and interest of anyone he felt an attraction to and wanted to get to know. Satya, for example. But he still wasn't sure if she was real or a dream. He was happy to explore any and all possibilities. If she was a dream, so be it. If she was real, where was she? He would sleep on it and hope for a resolution come morning.

CHAPTER FOUR

Off the Mountain

Ten rings, then voice mail. Max didn't want to wait to talk to Lea, so he revved up his all white Justin Bieber Special Edition Vespa and drove south toward Ubud and the home they shared. The home he hoped to keep sharing with her if he could convince her he was worth it.

The Vespa was a wedding gift from his brother Barry, and he loved driving it. The odds of his brother ever coming back to Bali were both slim and none, but nonetheless, he decided against painting over the Justin Bieber nametag painted on the fuel tank. He could live with the occasional heckling. He owed at least that much to his brother. If he was going to accept the gift, accept all of it.

On the plus side, the bike was faster and heavier than the little Scooby Scooters that clogged every street and alleyway in Ubud and the rest of Bali. He felt much safer on it. If you didn't want to drive a scooter or walk, Bali was not the best choice. There were other fabulous islands like Gili T, where there are no motorized vehicles at all. The only noise and commotion there came from tourists having too much fun.

For now, here he was, driving with his helmet on, eye guard flipped down, and leaning right and left as he took the turns like A.J. Floyd or Parnelli Jones.

Their villa is actually in an area called Penestanan. It's a smaller village next to Ubud, just as Beverly Hills is next to Los Angeles. It sits at a slightly higher elevation offering unique views of the forest and rice fields, and is home to many of the more chic restaurants, galleries, and boutiques the wealthier tourists and better-funded digital nomads seek out.

It was an area Max knew about, but until Dori came into his life, it was one he was only able to enjoy for the occasional night out or for an overpriced coffee with a friend. To be sure, the price tag was not designed for backpackers. But, at this moment, it wouldn't have mattered to Max where his villa was. His only concern was how quickly he could get there.

So many choices, so many decisions and the constant irony of the tricks the mind plays. He'd gone to bed thinking about Satya, but woke up thinking about Lea. After the conversation and insight he'd gained from his meeting with Satya, imaginary or real, he felt motivated and clear as he took the white knuckle turns toward his villa.

He wanted to ask Lea for a chance to prove he could let his walls down and be an open and equal partner in their relationship. Every mile on the bumpy, winding road, he thought about how he could make amends. The closer he got, the more he wanted to see her lounging around in one of her free-flowing button down night shirts or one of his extra-large T-shirts she loved wearing after they made love. The mental vision aroused him. He could just imagine the thin bamboo fabric clinging to her breasts outlining their perfect shape, falling loosely just below her waist to the top of her bum — every movement a tantalizing invitation to intimacy.

He hoped she would fall into his arms so they'd be like two lovers in a movie scene the moment he walked in — the "you had me at hello" fantasy. His mouth opened slightly, involuntarily, as he drove, as he was kissing her in his mind, imagining her body wrapped around his. The splat of huge Bali mosquitos against the eye shield of his helmet were no deterrence. He merely hoped they were not an omen to the obstacles before him. *Ganesha, where are you?*

When he finally pulled into their flower filled and landscaped circular driveway, he noticed another scooter parked next to Lea's Honda. When he turned the doorknob to enter, Lea's friend Ingrid was walking toward him from the kitchen. "Hi, Max. She's out back."

Ingrid was always in a world of her own. She retired at the age of thirty after selling her meditation start-up to the venture capital group that funded her in the first place for a big payday. She was more ethereal than third dimension physical beauty, but by whatever label you called her physical presence, she had some kind of allure that turned the heads of men and women equally.

Max was drawn to her for the same reasons most others were, but he and his ego were spared any potential rejection for a couple of reasons. One, he was living with her best friend. And two, the opportunity had already come and gone and he passed whatever kind of test to his willpower one would say it was. It made him look much more confident and desirable in Ingrid's eyes than he actually felt, but *she* didn't know that. In her eyes, he had maybe the tiniest bit of aloofness that she mistook for self-confidence.

She was like a walking pheromone, presenting a challenge to him whenever she came by to visit Lea. It was one thing to see her in the kitchen making tea wearing her long see-through yoga pants and another challenge entirely when she would slide her yoga pants down and walk naked to the hot tub. Max would look on with the envy of a teenager when she would slide over the edge of the hot tub and hug Lea with the warmth and affection of soul mates. He was never sure if she did that to mess with him or if she was just that free in body, mind and spirit. It didn't really matter. It was nice to see.

Max was not distracted by her presence. He looked around and saw a carry-on style travel bag with one of Lea's sweaters and a purse resting on top. Not getting a reply from Max, Ingrid continued toward the front door. "I guess I'll leave you two to whatever it is," she said. And with that, Ingrid walked out.

Lea heard the voices once she put down her garden hose. She walked into the kitchen just as Ingrid had her hand on the doorknob. Ingrid looked directly at her close friend and said, "Call me."

"Will do. Talk to you later," she said to Ingrid's back as her friend walked out the door and closed it behind her.

"What was that all about?" he asked with squinted eyes, visibly flustered.

"I'm going to India with Ingrid. We're taking a three-week retreat at Parmarth Niketan in Rishikesh."

Max didn't say anything. His eyes went to Lea's packed bag and lingered there while he gathered his thoughts.

"It's where Ingrid did her yoga teacher training," Lea added. "She also helped them set up their software and website, which apparently needs some attention. Anyway, she invited me to come with her and she set me up in some great yoga classes and a private room at the ashram while she works. I'll have a safe place to stay and when her work is done we're going to explore."

Max wasn't sure if his facial expression revealed what his monkey mind was telling him. As nice and cheerful as Ingrid could be, he always thought of her as nothing but sweet trouble. To make matters worse, there was nothing he could do about it. Ingrid and Lea were a bonded pair who once shared a flat in Perth, Australia, as well as a mutual desire to move to Bali together and find their spiritual life.

He had to smile a little. That's not an uncommon reason for moving to Bali.

"Now? You want to leave now?" he asked. "I was gone one night. I woke up and raced home because I want to be with you. I mean, really be with you. You told me to figure things out. I did."

"Life is funny, you always say. I figured a few things out as well, right here in our beautiful garden. It's time I followed my heart. I need something more. I'm not sure what it is, but I'll know it when I find it. You will too, Max."

"So, you feel right now is a good time to leave with Ingrid? Is this her idea?"

"Maybe, a little bit. We bounce ideas off each other all the time. Sometimes she knows what I need more than I do."

"That's really hard for me to believe," he said skeptically.

"Well, believe it or not. We both know something is missing. What we have is nice, don't get me wrong. But I don't want nice in this sense. Nice is for a weather report. And if I'm being honest, I'm tired of the ease with which we both ignore this."

Max ran his fingers through his hair to help him think. "This is not what I expected to come home to."

"Let me finish, Max. I wasn't planning to have this conversation now, but I'm ready if you are. And by the way, you have no right to have expectations of me now or any time. Do you get that?"

This was a version of Lea he'd never seen. She was making him face some truths he probably wasn't ready for. At least until it was his idea.

"You're right." He took a seat on the sofa. Lea sat next to him. He continued. "So, tell me what else you thought about."

"For starters, I want a life filled with passionate sex and hysterical laughter. I deserve it. I want to find you in the hot tub and see you look at me like you can't believe I'm yours. That's what I want."

Max took a few seconds. He got it. "I hope you know that I think you're gorgeous and sexy and amazing. And I do feel so lucky to have you in my life."

"I believe you, Max. I really do. But somewhere as the days have passed between us, we have settled into an easy friendship with occasional sex. I could live by myself if that's all I wanted. I want more than a roommate."

Max became very subdued. He knew she was right about almost everything. "I'm feeling very selfish now, Lea. I was… I am happy with a great roommate. You are so amazing. I don't like being alone as much as I pretend to and you keep me from that. I honestly didn't know you wanted so much more. I thought we loved each other in a way that meant we accepted each other as we are."

"I do love you and accept you the way you are. The sex complicates it, Max. I can't have this kind of random sex where there is no real love behind it. You will never love me the way you loved Dori, and that will never go away. The feelings I want to feel are not going to come from you. At the beginning, I let myself think they might. And that's on me."

Max couldn't think of a more uncomfortable conversation he'd ever had. The more Lea explained herself, the more he realized she was right on the money. He felt miserable.

"I don't know what to say. I feel terrible. Why didn't you say something before now?"

"There were many times I wanted to, and a few times I started to. In the end, I didn't say anything. I know you feel some of what I'm feeling and expressing to you. I can see it in your actions. Not all the time. There are moments where everything feels normal, like at the start, and it's those moments where we laugh and play that I feel connected with you in the way that I was when I first moved in. That's why I'm still here.

"But lately, we are so careful with each other. It feels like we're trying too hard to not mess anything up, rather than trusting each other enough to talk about what we're each going through."

"I'm really sorry Lea. You're truly a beautiful woman inside and out. I've been so blessed that you found me. Whatever I did to deserve you, I hope I can keep doing it."

"Thank you, Max. That may be the sweetest thing you ever said to me. You know, I've felt an attraction to you since the kirtan days of Max Talks two years ago. And it wasn't your singing voice. I miss those days. They were honest and open and were the foundation of our friendship. We've both changed since then, but we didn't let each other in on the changes."

Max took a deep breath and let it all out. Lea smiled immediately, because she knew what was coming. She loved Max's big breaths. She could read them like a shaman reads the coffee beans.

"Is it too late to re-start? I had the strangest night up on the mountain and when I woke up, I couldn't get here fast enough to talk to you. I've got the dead bugs on my helmet to prove it."

"I would love to hear about it when I return. There's a lot I've kept to myself and I owe you the whole story. I love you, but I think some time apart will give us the perspective we each need. Who knows, Max? Things change all the time. Let's allow the right thing to happen for each of us."

Max let out another huge sigh. He saw the red in Lea's eyes and could feel the truth in her words along with all the emotion of it. "I'm going to take a shower and lie down a bit. That ride down the mountain is not getting any easier. Will you be here a while longer?"

"Yes. I've got a few more things to get together. I'll make some tea for us for after your shower."

Max smiled as best he could. He knew the seriousness of her tone and he would not try to change her mind. He went into their bathroom and used up every last drop of hot water standing under the pulsing showerhead. When he was done, he toweled off and got under the sheets on their bed, falling asleep to some Nirinjan Kaur music. He loved her voice, in particular her ode to Guru Ram Das was a lullaby that always put him to sleep before the first chorus was over.

Lea came into the bedroom holding a bamboo tray with two cups of steaming hot tea and a small bowl of fruit. She saw he was sound asleep. She set the tray down on the nightstand and wrote a short note. She then put two freshly picked frangipani flowers from the garden on each side of the tray. After a long look at her sleeping friend, she kissed him gently on the forehead and said, "See you when I get back, my dear Max. Sweet dreams."

CHAPTER FIVE

Entitled Spiritualists

Morning is never late in Bali. It was either his internal clock or the sweet songbirds outside his window that marked the start of another day. Max looked over the note from Lea one last time. He slow walked into the kitchen and dropped the short note in the recycle bin under the sink. It was time to make the first cup of coffee. It was a favorite morning ritual and one that allowed him to gather his thoughts and set his intentions for the day.

He usually listened to morning mantras or even a short talk on how to start your day from the well-known Indian philosopher and teacher B.K. Shivani before he got out of bed. Once the day started, it was often hard for him to get back to that mindset. She had beautiful posts on Youtube that laid out simple but powerful words to start any day — words of gratitude, thankfulness, and intentions. Today, the coffee ritual would have to do.

It wasn't long after his first cup of dark roast, single origin Sumatran that he decided it would be a good time to spend a week at Om Ham. *There's no reason to sit alone in the villa. Why sulk when I can have company and a swimming pool to play in? I might even get lucky and see the Guru tending to his garden.*

He knew the guru well, but had not spoken to him in a while. He was mad at himself for that, but only when he thought about it. He was well aware, that whatever he was thinking, the Guru was already ahead of him. Best of all, he knew he could take comfort in knowing the Guru did not judge him for his actions. Whether it was a day, a week or a month since they talked, Master Ketut would be happy to see him and hopefully share a table and a bit of the wisdom he so generously passes on to all who ask or are within earshot.

He grabbed his white sarong and prayer beads. It was time to revisit the ashram, get a little cave therapy and leave the rest up to mother nature and all the infinite possibilities in life.

Max parked his scooter in the last available space at the end of the driveway. He walked under the big arch leading into Om Ham, greeted as usual by the ominous half smile of Hanuman, and soon after the always-smiling face of Govin, a long-time employee at Om Ham who had survived the Covid pandemic with his health intact. He and his family survived by eating a lot of rice, working hard, and keeping their faith in the gods that surround them at home and everywhere else on the island.

Multiple daily offerings at temples are a constant in Bali, and if a person was running late, there were ample places at Om Ham to get your prayers in. The salary the few regulars were paid during this time was a meager five U.S. dollars per day. Now that the pandemic was over, it was back up to seven.

When Max thought about this, it irked him to no end, especially when he thought about the staggering amount of petty complaining most Americans do over what is basically nothing, compared to the daily love and kindness offered to all by the people of Bali. These people know how to find their love and happiness in family, prayer, and work.

"Selamat Paggi, Mr. Max. It's good to see you. We are all happy for you to be here. How long you stay?"

"Thank you, Govin. I'm not sure yet, but at least a week. Is room 302 available?"

"Yes, Mr. Max. It is ready for you now. Gopi will bring your tea. Your massage with Indra is at two."

"Perfect. Terima Kasih (thank you). See you later, Govin."

"See you," Govin replied.

In all his time in Bali, Max still grappled with learning the language. It was way past time to be able to say more than hello and thank you.

Room 302 was the second largest room at Om Ham. It came equipped with a beautiful marble bathtub and separate shower. It also had a big balcony that looked out at the rice fields on one side and the village of Taman on the other. On a really clear day, there was even a view of the ocean if you were tall enough or didn't mind climbing a ladder. It was perfect.

This was the room he'd shared with Dori until they got married and moved into their villa. It held a lot of good memories for him, and as things would eventually turn out, Dori was not only one who created memories there.

Max was happy he'd come back to Om Ham. Indra gave him a great massage, and after a short swim, he was relaxed and tired enough to call it a day. He collapsed on his patio lounger, looking out at the setting sun.

There was a cool breeze coming in from the mountains which brought with it the very real possibility of an imminent thunderstorm. He loved falling asleep to the sounds of hard rain and the occasional clap of accompanying thunder. It was as good or better than any mantra he could have put on.

Time always went by fast at Om Ham. There were either friends he made on past visits who were back again, or there were new friends to be made. It was a beautiful cycle. Old friends showing up and new friends who would become old friends.

The days flew by, filled with swimming, talking, doing yoga and enjoying the abundance of peace and good vibes. It was nice having the dining room right there as well. With Lea gone, he was not up for cooking as much as when she was there to share the meals with him.

His first night back, was just what he needed. He woke up strong, hungry, and filled with energy, so he walked right over to the Tulsi Dining Room. He perused the buffet, but nothing really stood out. It was an all too familiar comment that was whispered about here and there amongst frequent guests. It was nice for newcomers, but after a while, bbq chicken wings and two different rice dishes along with the same assortment of breads and fruits were not a match for what he wanted.

There was an easy solution to something that was not really a problem. He walked over to the kitchen and politely asked for something his taste buds were craving. One dish was Nasi Goring, a plate of fried rice with either meat or vegetables and sweet and sour sauces over a bed of steamed red rice.

Number two on his Indonesian list of musts, was Gado-Gado. Along with being fun to say, it's versatile and delicious and has the ability to cure anyone of a dislike of vegetables. It can be made with meat, but the main component of a tasty gado-gado is the peanut sauce. Max loved his with tofu or tempeh. It's also generally served with a hardboiled egg or two on top of the traditional white rice.

On his more American feeling days, his standby breakfast was poached eggs on top of sourdough toast that was covered with fresh avocado and capers.

Breakfast in Bali. He smiled every time he thought about it.

Max decided to do some laps in the pool to work off his oversized appetite. *I haven't felt that hungry since Lea left.* He laughed out loud as soon as he thought that. She'd only been gone a day after all. He hoped that was a good sign.

His good mood lasted about a minute. Before he could park his butt in a shade covered lounge chair, he heard the scratchy voice of Deborah Willis, his third-floor neighbor from a while ago. He tried to ignore her as he laid down his towels, but her voice became louder and louder until she came directly into his line of vision. Her voice was like fingernails on a chalkboard or the yowling of cats in heat.

"Hi, Max. Remember me?"

"How could I forget you?" Max replied. "It's only been a year, and I stopped taking drugs a long time ago." *So much for living in the 5th dimension,* he thought. His old Chicago sarcasm had come back too fast for him to stop it. But the devil in him was happy. He winced and smiled a smile that belied his true feelings. *Hope I didn't sound as irritated as I actually feel,* he thought. *Elephants have long memories, you know.*

"Hi, Deborah. Are you still living here?"

"Of course. Where else would I be?"

Of course, Max thought sarcastically. He had an answer for where he'd like her to be, but he was trying really hard to be kind. *It's not supposed to be hard to be kind. It doesn't cost any extra,* his mother would always say. "It's nice to see you again, Deborah. How are you?"

She went on as if he was interested.

If only I acted that well when auditioning for TV roles in my earlier life.

"I still go to the Pyramids of Chi every week and I keep in touch with my channeling trance group."

"That's so nice," Max replied half-heartedly. "It's good to have a steady routine, keep all the distractions at bay." *I'm trying,* he thought miserably.

"I don't get distracted. I thought you would know that by now. Anyway, as you know, I'm very good friends with the Guru. In fact, I have an appointment with him in ten minutes. He lets me pop in to see him whenever I'm here."

"Well, nice of you to say hi, Deborah. I'm going to finish off my laps. Have a great day. It's nice to see you and hear that life is going so well for you."

Before Deborah could reply, Max pushed off the edge of the pool. He immediately went under the surface to swim to the other side. His reaction to her bothered him on more than one level. There was the basic level of just not liking her. But then, there was the honesty of realizing that when we project qualities we don't like about other people, they are often the things we don't like about ourselves. Maybe he was the one walking around with a look of entitlement. So many lessons, so little time. Or as they are now called, opportunities. Lessons are from the ego. Opportunities are from the heart. He knew where he wanted to operate from and what he had to do to live it. "Just do it," says the slogan on the tennis shoes.

With that for motivation, he went back to floating on the crystal clear water of the famous Om Ham swimming pool. He could hear guests talking about when they arrived and how much they loved being there. He was happy for them and all the magic that was now at their fingertips. He looked up at the blue sky… "Sorry everyone."

CHAPTER SIX

Max and Alexandra

The pool at Om Ham was still Max's saving grace. It was early enough to hear some roosters crowing from the neighboring yards, but the sun was already high enough to shine on the full length of the pool's crystal-clear water. He did laps until his arms were too tired to reach out in front of him.

With his remaining strength, he floated over to the shallow end and rested against the steps, still half in the water. It was a favorite position of his, allowing him to stay cool and refreshed, while at the same time adding a layer of tan to his ever-darkening skin tone.

It didn't slip his mind that it was also much easier to begin a conversation with someone who was already in a playful state as compared to someone lying on a towel with her nose in a book. *Life is good,* he thought. I'm happy where I am. Other than scattered white puffs here and there, the clouds were gone. It was a perfect day.

Om Ham was the extent of his socializing these days. He had stopped doing his Max Talks groups at Sayuri and it had already been a few months since he enjoyed a kirtan session. Something was brewing that he could not put his finger on. But, there was also something that was easy for him to identify. He was enjoying seeing beautiful women at the pool. It felt good to feel less inhibited about making eye contact with someone he found attractive. He was having fun and he decided he would make the best of being on his own if the opportunity presented itself.

Feeling thirsty after his swim, he gestured toward the kitchen. Gopi saw him waving from her station in the dining room and guessed correctly that he wanted a coconut. She brought it over to the table next to him with the top cut off, a spoon attached at the side, and a bamboo straw inside. He walked up the two steps at the shallow end of the pool and sat down at the edge of his lounge chair to enjoy his elixir.

Just as he leaned in for his first sip of the sweet, hydrating coconut water, he heard a voice. As his eyes drifted from his drink, he saw sandals on the ground next to his chair. Red painted toenails peeked out at the front end of blue flip flops. "Does everyone around here get that kind of service?" The voice was soft, sexy and pleasant.

Trying hard not to stare at the long, tan legs in front of him, Max looked higher. Although the glaring sun blocked the woman's face, his eyes were already fixed on the tattoos over both of the woman's shoulders. They were red, blue and black ink drawings depicting Shiva, Hanoman, and Ganesha. *Satya?* he wondered? The woman pulled a lounge chair close to him and sat down.

"May I join?" she asked in a soft Russian accent. "I'm Alexandra."

"Hi. Yes, that would be great. I'm Max." He nodded at his coconut and asked, "Would you like one?"

"Thank you. It looks good," she replied as she sat down next to him.

Max waved a friendly hello back to Gopi. When she noticed him, he motioned at the coconut with his index finger held high. She understood his basic sign language, which was much better than his basic Indonesian Bahasa, and brought over another coconut. It was cut at the top, with a bamboo straw inside and a spoon attached at the side just like his.

Attempting a bit of humor, Max said "If this was a bar in California, I would probably ask you if you come here often."

"Thankfully, this is not a bar in California," she said. "If I heard a cheesy line like that, I would take my coconut and find another chair."

"Good thing coconuts are easy to come by around here," Max answered rather quickly.

"Ha," Alexandra said, and cracked a smile.

That comeback was spontaneous and real. Much better. Maybe he'll be worth the effort, she thought. She liked older men, and could tell from a distance there was something about this one that was intriguing. He seemed a bit aloof, but in a nice way. He was also fit for his age. Fifty something she was guessing, which was fine with her.

Her first lover was 37 when she was an exchange student living in Paris. Gilber, the brother of the husband of the family who was sponsoring her, was tall with wavy, dark hair and bright blue eyes. His smile was wide and happy and he fit the persona of a lover who would be good in bed and not in a hurry to leave afterwards.

She was only seventeen then, but not a virgin. Even so, she considered Gilber her first lover, because losing her virginity at a senior prom dance was not anything close to what she imagined a real lover to be like.

This was Paris. The place where husbands *and* wives each had lovers. It was the city of lights. A place where exploring sex was not a taboo to run from but a pleasure to run toward.

To her, Max felt warm and at ease with himself. She was only here for a night and she enjoyed these kinds of private moments where she could let go and be free from the admonishing, judgmental eyes of friends back home. Furthermore, this was Bali. It would be her "eat, pray, love" night without the eating and the praying. Her mind was made up. She would find out if her new friend was up to the task.

"Did you just get here?" Max asked with a hopeful smile.

"I arrived late last night. I didn't get much sleep, so, here I am. Swimming is a good way to wake up, don't you think?"

"I love swimming, Max replied. Om Ham is my home away from home, and this pool is a big reason for that. There's a lot to do here. How long are you staying?"

"Unfortunately, just tonight. I'm meeting some girlfriends in Nusa Pineda for scuba and snorkeling. Do you know that place?"

"Yes. It's beautiful. Some say that is where you will see the best sunsets in all of Bali. Are you leaving from the port at Padang Bai?"

"Yes, that's it. I'd forgotten the name already. My friends are in Ubud and we will all meet at the port tomorrow. I forget which day it is with all the time changes."

"Ha. That's a good sign. Happens all the time. Happily, it hardly matters here."

The conversation flowed as they drank from their coconuts and shared some travel stories. Alexandra was strikingly beautiful and well spoken. Her long, blond hair fell neatly over her shoulders to the middle of her back. Her turquoise bikini was cut across the top at an angle, leaving little to the imagination. The thong bottom was nothing more than a fig leaf in the front and what had to be a somewhat uncomfortable string between her cheeks serving as the rest of the swimsuit.

Every time she moved forward to sip her juice, Max's eyes went along for the ride. She was not only beautiful, but she was smart and was on a six-month holiday traveling all over Southeast Asia. He was a bit envious and taken in by all of it.

Alexandra talked about her first trip to Thailand and how much she loved it. As it often happens in life, something we first consider to be tragic or unfortunate, turns out to be the best thing that ever happened to us. This was the case with Alexandra.

Her mother took her on a beautiful holiday to the exotic islands of Phuket and Koh Phi Phi. During their first week, however, her mother fell ill and had to be taken to a local hospital. Once there, it became evident the language barrier was a problem. Her mother only spoke Russian and the doctors were scrambling to find a go-between.

Alexandra stepped right in to interpret, and after all was said and done, she was offered a job in Thailand at the same hospital as an interpreter. Thailand was a common Russian holiday location and her services would be put to use for as long as she wanted and as soon as she was available.

When she first arrived with her mom as a tourist, she was young and broke. In this twist of life, or fate if you will, her future was forever changed. She had been living there for four years now, earning a great salary and living the life she'd always hoped for. She told Max she would fly her mother there to be with her soon.

The story drew him in for so many reasons. It was powerful, romantic and showed the promise of life that he loved believing in. He had not been to Thailand yet, and now he knew he must go. *Maybe Bali has served its purpose.* That thought surprised him. He never believed he would say something like that. Even to himself.

Alexandra settled in the small island of Koh Phi Phi, and spent her days teaching yoga, swimming in the soft, blue waters and scuba diving and snorkeling. She enjoyed her life to the fullest. *Maybe there would be magic there for me as well,* Max thought as Alexandra continued.

The more he heard, the more he was attracted to her. He was listening more than talking for a change. She was smart, funny, direct and knew what she wanted out of life. He was excited in so many ways.

When the air shifted, she pulled a few things from her purse to slip into. Even in simple brown shorts and a plain white t-shirt, she was beautiful. She wore a magical looking pendant on a silver necklace that dropped just to the top of her chest. He could hardly take his eyes off it.

She said it was made by a friend of hers who lived in Bali, no less. Max couldn't believe it. He had been here a few years already and had never come across something so beautiful. The pendant was handmade and the artist drew upon the buyers birthday, age and life intention.

It fit Alexandra's long neck as if it were made just for her. The power and beauty of it was the perfect match for her personality. She was happy to share the artist's name and Instagram account, sensing Max would like one for himself.

Max know the artist would be his next phone call.

Eventually, the sun started its slow descent and along with it came a slight drizzle from the darkening sky above.

"Shall we get out of the rain?" Max asked hopefully.

Alexandra grabbed a lace shawl from her purse and draped it over her shoulders. "That would be lovely," she replied.

They walked up the steps to his room. As they passed the reception area, Max felt the piercing eyes of the Guru fall on his shoulders. The Guru was busy working on his garden. He pulled weeds and planted fruits, and during Covid, when Om Ham was mostly empty, he did the engraving on all the stone steps leading around the retreat. It was his home, business and the place he invested his life's blood and energy in.

He met all the guests personally, as many were there specifically to see him for a bodywork treatment or spiritual session. It was the main attraction that Om Ham advertised when they were listed on various travel sites, boasting a yoga retreat with healing programs.

The Guru knew Max, Dori and Lea on a far more personal level than just about any other guest, most of whom were only there for a week, never to be seen again. For this reason, it did not give him any pleasure to see Max give in to the same weakness time and time again.

The had Guru put so much of his time into trying to help Max make wiser decisions, and be more spiritual as he often he wanted to be. But, you can only lead a horse to water, as the old saying goes.

Being the wise man that he was, the Guru knew Max did not have the internal makeup to be a devotee or follower of anyone. His own will was too strong. That was one reason that could be given, the other was that he was afraid of total surrender. Max was not the type of person who would be in a crowd of feet kissing followers pushing towards the front of the line to bow at the altar of the presiding mystic.

He would follow any wise man or spiritual leader to a degree, but with a cutoff point if he found himself chanting with a group of people whose eyes were glazed over in pure adulation. "We are all just human beings," he would tell himself. "No one person is above another." Yet the Guru knew that Max hoped to attain, those same mystical qualities that the enlightened few honor in themselves. He also knew that Max felt if he had to kiss the feet of one of these mystics, he would fall short of his goals. His damn ego always got in his way.

All of these personal choices were of no consequence to the Guru. He was not looking for blind followers who wanted someone to do their thinking for them. Guru Ketut Arsana loved Max for who he was and liked that he did not pretend to be someone else.

Max didn't spend much time at the ashram meditating in the caves or dressing in white for the monthly ceremonies, yet he carried himself with an awareness or consciousness that attracted many people to him. The Guru even loved Max for this quality and probably teased him too often about how he needed a young woman to make him feel whole again. The Guru's words had obviously hit home.

Max's easy charm and self-assurance was picked up on by a beautiful young woman and it didn't take much more than her friendly hello to get his heart pumping. The Guru would not be pushing so hard in the future.

When Max closed the door to his room, he turned around to see that Alexandra had already dropped her shorts and bikini to the floor. She walked naked to the shower, slowly and confidently. She was neither shy nor modest, and seemed as comfortable without her clothes as she was sitting by the pool drinking her coconut water.

"Do you mind," she asked as she opened the shower stall door.

"No," Max said quickly.

"Join me," she said invitingly as she disappeared behind the frosted glass.

Max dropped his suit to the floor next to hers and caught up with her as the steaming water started pouring down over her slim, tan body. Her breasts were upright and nearly completely tanned, with barely a trace of white skin highlighting her state of arousal. She reached for his hands and pulled him under the mist of the rainforest spray shower head with her.

He wrapped his arms around her and kissed her passionately. She smelled like flowers. He kissed her breasts, first one, then the other. She was a free spirit, and her body responded without a trace of inhibition.

Feeling his own freedom, he let his left hand move down from her breasts. His fingertips caressed her, moving slowly over her body to the soft mound below her tummy, then down between her inner thighs.

He could feel her desire through the warm water that covered them. Her legs parted in anticipation, just enough for him to linger until she asked for more without saying a word. She pulled his face to hers and they embraced each other's desires with abandon.

CHAPTER SEVEN

Divine Synchronicity

Alexandra was gone, but the memory of her lingered. The sheets smelled of a heavenly mix of their mutual passion and the subtle fragrance she wore on her skin. Max inhaled deeply and let his head drop back onto his soft down filled pillow. He wanted to savor as much as he could. Aroma therapy at its best. He had no plans for the day and a bit more sleep seemed like a good idea. Even the nearby roosters cooperated.

In his semi dream like state of mind, memories of his first California girlfriend, Jennifer Bloom, took front and center. A half smile parted his lips when he said her last name. Bloom. When they met, that was exactly what she was. A blossoming flower. He couldn't help but wonder what the Jennifer Bloom of today would be like. Alexandra reminded him of her and now he wondered where she was in the world. Like Alexandra, she had long hair that went down to the middle of her back. Hers was a dirty blonde that curled naturally. She had soft pale skin, light blue eyes, and a smile that revealed a curiosity of life in every way. She looked both innocent and seductive all at once. And like Alexandra, she was a free spirit willing to follow a whim on any particular day. Her figure was slim, but not without curves she was proud and free in her mind to show off. She couldn't fathom a reason to wear a bra or cover up what God gave her. Being a nudist at heart, he was in heaven. And on more than once occasion, he would recall how she encouraged his attention to her body.

They met when he was thirty one, teaching night school in Simi Valley, California. She was an east coast transplant, barely twenty and unsure of where to live or what to do. She landed at his night school program as part of a deal with her parents in exchange for housing at a friend of theirs who lived near the school.

Max felt an instant attraction. He wasn't sure if it was anything more than sexual, but he wanted to find out. He enjoyed her curiosity of life and the passion she had for new experiences. She was an old soul in the sense that she was not particular about the age of someone who struck her fancy. That was like kryptonite for him. He was an old soul as well and he found comfort in meeting others with that DNA. He could laugh about that now, as his spiritual growth was teaching him that being an old soul was not necessarily a mark of greatness, but rather a sign of slow learner. Who said learning about ourselves with the intention to be better, would be easy? The misconceptions we take on in our youth that make us feel so good, fade away like the illusion of time the farther along our path we go.

They met when he went into his school office to do some work on the attendance records before locking up for the night. She was lying on the corner love seat, barefoot, with her feet resting on a pillow. Her head turned when she heard the door open and close.

"Hi. I wasn't expecting to find anyone in here. Are you okay? Do you go here?"

"Kinda okay and yes, I go here. My name is Jennifer."

"Hi Jennifer. My name is Max Simon. I teach the night school program here. Are you not feeling well?"

"My stomach feels upset, but otherwise, I'm fine. I just came in to rest. Are you the teacher I am supposed to register with?"

"May I?" Max asked gently as he walked to sit down on the sofa next to a now upright Jennifer. She smiled and nodded in approval and before they even noticed, a couple of hours passed and the rest of the school emptied out. Their chemistry was instantaneous on all levels. Jennifer sat close enough so that their knees were touching and her left arm was leaning against his right. They talked until her host arrived to pick her up and had already made plans to connect again soon. School or elsewhere. Max hoped for elsewhere.

He wasn't quite sure what to make of it all at first, so their first few dates were coffee and talking. Their age difference, while only eleven years, led to many interesting conversations about life and love. One night in particular, they chatted over coffee oblivious to the time. The Insomnia Cafe in Sherman Oaks was closing and they had to leave. Jennifer explained that it was too late for her to disturb her host family, and asked if she could spend the night at his place.

That night was the first of many at his place. Two weeks later she moved into Max's bedroom at a big home he shared with another man and woman. They lived in a place called Topanga Canyon, high in the hills above Malibu beach in a live and let live kind of community. It was home to many famous bands of the time. Electric Light Orchestra, Little Feet, a few members of the Byrds, and the occasional Neil Young sighting at the local bar called The Corral. There was a pool table, saw dust on the floor and the obligatory drunken brawl every so often. Drugs and sex flowed freely.

Their relationship didn't last long, but it was sweet, fun and safe. There was no harm done other than to Max's ego when she would disappear for a couple of days at a time. Even though he fully understood the challenges of dating a young woman who was in a very exploratory time of her life, it still hurt. He knew that for a fact, because on one of their weekend away trips, he thumbed through her diary to see if there was anything of interest about him. What he did see, was a quote that helped him realize his time was coming to an end. She wrote about her interest in travel and men, with the quote "So many men, so little time." Ha. This from an eighteen year old according to the date on the bottom of the page. He could only imagine what she would write now that she was turning twenty one soon. He loved her for who she was. She gave him a certain kind of freedom that is not easy to find. The freedom to be himself. She gave him memories that would last a lifetime. Sweet dreams, Jennifer. Wherever you are.

CHAPTER EIGHT

Past Present Future

Max sat stoically in the stone hot tub just outside the double French doors of the master bedroom at his villa. It was built into the deck, above ground, as a wedding present from the Guru and featured a small Ganesha face carved into the side facing the bedroom. There was a colorful tile infinity symbol on the bottom, similar to the larger one at the Om Ham pool. The Guru was an artist in every sense of the word. His canvas was the garden, the pool, anywhere he could make a place look and feel more beautiful. Max didn't use the spa often, but it seemed to be the perfect time and place to be still and think about all that transpired in the last few days. The water in the spa was not the only thing bubbling up.

He sipped his morning coffee while his mind went to the night with Alexandra and the day dreams of Jennifer. He had more thoughts running through his mind than he was comfortable with. White Herons and huge black butterflies flew overhead. Their grace was a constant reminder of the beauty of nature and the power of the universe that was just outside his bedroom door. Amidst it all, however, he was trying to figure out a path forward and what, if anything, the past week would do to influence that path.

His body was relaxed from the 103-degree water. The handful of lavender bath salts he threw in added to his quiet state of mind. He flipped open his MacBook tablet carefully placed on the deck to protect it from the steam and water. He wanted to look at old photos and check his Facebook posts and notifications. The long-forgotten memories of Jennifer made him wonder about her and a few of the other women in his past that stood out for one reason or another. He wondered where they were, what happened to them, and what happened between them that led to such short-term relationships.

There was one woman in particular, Joi, that caused him the most angst. She was one year below him at Von Steuben High School in Chicago. In his last year of college at NIU University in DeKalb, Illinois, she became his first honest to goodness lover. They both still lived at home and as this was before cell phones and the instant text saying the coast was clear, they worked in harmony to make the most of each opportunity. Once they had a room to themselves, they played silly sexual games that only youthful energy and newcomers to adult fun could appreciate. Games like having sex and then watching the clock to see how many minutes it would take before he was hard enough to have sex again. They were too young to care that the time *between* sex was always a lot long longer than the time *during* sex.

He kept a photo of her in his wallet since the day it was recovered much like a fossil from an archeological dig. Although this time, it was merely a box of old photos his mom saved for the sake of saving. It was one of those high school graduation style photos, wallet size, black and white, with a note on the back written from the person in the photo to the person it was being given to. In this case, it was from Joi, to Max. On the back were the simple, but powerful words, "To Max. My best friend and love of my life. My Soulmate forever." Love, Joi.

Memory lane was good. It was also short-lived. Max heard the wind chimes from the front door and then the wispy King's English voice of Ingrid as she moved closer to him. She could see his white hair and unmistakable bald spot while the rest of him was submerged.

"Hi, Max. Mind if I get in?" She disrobed without waiting for an answer and slid her long legs over the edge into the steaming water.

He swiveled his head in her direction. "I have some news you may be interested in," she began.

Not getting much of a response, Ingrid reached across his chest to grab his wine glass as she dropped into the spa. She took a slow sip, then let her body slide all the way under for a moment. She came up with her interlocked fingers as high over her head as she could, then let out a long full breath as she lowered her hands and finally her bottom onto the tile next to him.

"So? You were saying?"

Ingrid hoped for more of a reaction to her long sensual body being right in Max's face. She would never do anything with him, of course, but her ego wanted to know if he would try. If she were being totally honest, she would admit she wanted to have sex with him. But since she couldn't, she felt it her total obligation to tease the hell out of him. *For Lea's sake,* she thought. *After all, what are friends for?*

"So, Maxie, Lea is still in India. She met up with a yoga teacher she had a romance with during her teacher training days. I didn't get details, but she did say they were taking the Toy Train from Kalka to Shimla and then hiring a guide to do some trekking along the Himalayas. After that, it's anyone's guess."

"And when is all this happening?" Max asked.

"I'm not really sure. This guy, Mobin something, still teaches and Lea still has a few weeks on her class program and a few other things she wants to do while she's there. We talked about Goa for a final weekend kind of thing. That's about it."

Max wanted to know more than that. "Did she mention anything about me?"

"I'm sorry, Max. It was a short conversation. That's pretty much the crux of it. She didn't tell me not to say anything, so either she wanted me to tell you or she didn't mind if I told you."

Max lifted himself out of the spa halfway, and sat up on the top step of the jacuzzi. He was silent for a moment, and he knew he needed to be alone.

"Ingrid, thank you. I appreciate you sharing the news from Lea, but I would like to sit here alone right now. Would you mind?"

Ingrid got up from the spa and took Max's empty wine glass with her. "Not at all. I know Lea loves you. Maybe she's waiting to know if *you* really love her. Take that leap of faith, Max. It could be the best thing you ever do in this lifetime." She didn't wait for an answer, as she grabbed her wrap and walked away.

CHAPTER NINE

Satya, Again

Max was motionless on his chaise lounge positioned next to the spa. The sun had finally dropped behind some of the tall Banyan trees surrounding his villa. His eyes were closed. An open book lay face down on the side table next to his lounger, alongside an empty Bintang bottle. He had a small hand towel covering his privates, that had protected him from the hot midday sun earlier in the day.

The skin on his arms had begun to tingle and he could feel goosebumps forming. It was an eerily familiar feeling. He looked up and suddenly her right hand was on his heart. The colored ink images of Shiva and Ganesha were the same as he remembered from his weekend on the mountain when this beautiful, mysterious woman appeared from the mist to sit with him. "Satya?"

"Yes, Max. I'm here for you. How may I help?"

Max blinked his eyes a few times and then opened them wide, unsure of what he would see. But she was still there. Satya was sitting next to him just like she did when he was watching the sunset on Mount Batur. When he'd been trying to clear his mind and get clarity on how to move forward, she had appeared out of the mist to give him advice and tell him he had to choose whether his life would it be with Lea or if he'd be on his own again. Now, he was back home in

Ubud facing the same but more urgent choice, and Satya was back. This time there was no mist.

The fact that he was experiencing a mystical / supernatural / spiritual moment was not unnerving for him. In the past few months, he'd been going deeper and deeper into his mind with powerful music played at frequencies that invited higher states of consciousness.

He was focused on moving from life in the third dimension to living in the fifth dimension and higher. The videos for this were readily available on YouTube and can be found by searching 999hz, 1111hz, and many more and by adding simple text in the search bar such as - connecting to your spirit guide or meditations for higher dimensions.

There are twelve dimensions available to us with the proper effort and focus, and Max felt happy enough to lock into what he had come to know as fifth dimension consciousness. But, he was not locked in long enough and thoroughly enough to stay there all the time. His dreams and his ability to contact his higher self and his spirit guides had improved dramatically though. And better still, the choices he made in his third dimensional mindset were becoming better. Being right or wrong in conversations was gone. Being trapped by the illusion of time, and saying *have to* was gone, replaced with *choose to*. Now, when these moments happened, he was happy and ready for them. Good-bye ego, he hoped!

"I'm confused again, Satya," Max started as if he were talking to an old friend. "I feel like I am in the same mental state I was in when we first met on the mountain."

Satya removed her hand from his heart and sat at the foot of the lounger.

"How long have you been here?" Max asked.

"You mean, did I hear your conversation with Ingrid? Yes, of course. I am always with you, Max. I hear everything."

"This doesn't seem real. Am I in a dream?" he wanted to know.

"Who's to say what's real and what is not?" Satya answered in an open-ended manner. "When I'm with you, it's real. You can call it whatever you want."

"I was doing a meditation to contact my higher self," he replied. I wasn't sure if I was asleep or not, and then I felt your hand."

"You have me, you have your higher self, you have your guides, angels and god," Satya continued, doing her best to reinforce his beliefs. "We all come to serve in different forms from time to time when the request is honest and pure from the heart."

"I'm unsure, Satya. I don't know what to do."

"Joi is from your past, Max. A long ago past, and there is nothing to be gained from looking for her, and even less in finding her. Go find Lea, if that is what your heart tells you. I can't tell you who to love, only not to be afraid of love. We are with you in spirit. Pun intended."

"Ha. So, spirit guides have a sense of humor?"

"Always. How else could we survive interactions with earthlings."

Max twisted around to the snack table to get his water bottle and in that instant, he felt a wisp of wind and a chill up and down his arms. When he turned back, she was gone.

CHAPTER TEN

Ali and Fleur

Max came out of the shower wrapped in his ultra-soft, long, white bathrobe. For him, it served the same purpose a newborn's favorite blanket. If Dori or Lea had allowed it, he would have worn it as part of his everyday apparel. He got it while on a long layover during one of his first flights to Bali. He'd opted to stay at the Hong Kong Airport Marriott where he'd stayed instead of spending sixteen hours trying to pass the time walking the terminals and gates window shopping and looking for a quiet place to take a nap.

It was a good move. The Marriott was gorgeous, and his hotel room was on the fourteenth floor with an expansive view of the nearby harbor and mountains. The bed was a tired traveler's dream and within seconds of getting out of his clothes, he was fast asleep. But, that was then.

Awake and ready to go, Max looked at the assorted piles of clothes he'd laid out, earlier trying to decide what to take. He wasn't sure how long he'd be gone, but he knew there was no reason to overpack. If he needed something, he could just buy it — goods and services were even cheaper in India than in Indonesia. The climate was also close to what he was used to in Bali — hot, humid, and miserable.

The surrounding nature and environment give or take a few different species of snakes and mosquitos was also pretty similar to many parts of Indonesia and Southeast Asia. He didn't know it as he packed, but the crowded streets of India would give him a new appreciation for Ubud and the traffic he often complained about.

Max stopped looking through his wardrobe and finally grabbed a handful of t-shirts, shorts, and other essentials to fill his backpack. *This is happening,* he thought. He decided to go forward as fast as possible before the illusion of fear could creep into his mind and change his direction. Thoughts of Lea and Joi bounced back and forth like a game of pickle ball in. his head. Instead of being a sweet, wonderful memory of a first love, the image of Joi rattled him a bit. *Maybe it's a good kind of rattle?* he wondered. *The kind that shakes a person out of the doldrums and into action. This is the right decision. I don't even remember Joi's last name.* That bothered him. He wondered how it was even possible. Every woman he knew remembered her first kiss. "Enjoy the beautiful memories and go find your girl." That's what the voice in his head told him and that's what he was going to do.

He looked around the villa one last time. Then, he called Ingrid and asked her to check on things every few days or so if she could. *Can't be too cautious. Even in Bali,* he thought.

Then, Max had an idea and made one last call before getting a taxi to the airport. His best option for while he was gone was to invite Fleur and Ali to come to Bali and stay in his villa to relax. He knew it would be great to see them when he returned, and he knew they would have a good time catching up with life at Om Ham and the ashram while he was gone. It was a win-win as they say.

The smiling, happy voice of Fleur finally picked up on the fourth ring. "Max. Hi. Wow! It's been a minute. How are you, dude?"

Max's mood shifted immediately. Fleur was as much his savior as he was hers when he saved her that first night. It felt like barely a second since their last conversation, and a minute since they laughed and made love together. *Time. We get so hung up on it, when in reality, it's really nothing but an illusion,* he thought. "I'm good. Is Ali around? I have something I want to talk to both of you about something."

"Yeah, sure. I'm switching over to video, so put your pants on. Okay? She joked, then said, "Hey, Ali, come to the kitchen. I'm on a video call with Max."

Max was smiling already, and happy he'd made the call. It was great to hear Fleur's voice. He was never really sure how things would be between them, but the moment she answered the phone, she sounded the same as always — sweet, friendly and interested in his life.

Ali walked into frame, and Max could see them both in full view. "Hey, stranger. It's great to hear from you. In fact, as I guess you can now see, Fleur and I have some news we wanted to share with you," he said, glancing at Fleur's baby bump. "What do you think?" Ali asked.

Max walked out his front door, closed it behind him, and sat down on the bench in front of the Ganesha sculpture. This was a call he needed to sit down for. Even seated with Ganesha by his side, he was stammering as he spoke. "This is amazing. Damn! When did this happen? How did this happen?"

"Well, Max, long story short, Fleur and I had a fight. She went out to a bar, got drunk and fucked a stranger."

"What? Fleur? Seriously, what is going on here?"

Fluer chimed in quickly. "The guy wasn't a total stranger."

Max was up off his bench and pacing. He was at a loss for words. Then he asked. "Are you okay? Do you need anything? I can come there?"

There was silence. Ali started to laugh. Then Fleur came to his rescue. "We're just messing with you, Maxie. We've been talking about it for a while, and after looking into the very best sperm banks, we finally made a choice and we're really happy it all worked out. We were hoping you would be totally, incredibly happy for us," Ali added.

"I sure wasn't expecting this kind of surprise. But it's awesome. Really. I love you both. I mean, I would have volunteered, you know. Nothing like old friends getting together for the common good, right?"

Fleur jumped in with passion. "Right. Glad to hear you're still a dreamer, Max."

"Yeah, yeah. Can't blame a guy for trying. Can I just share my news already?"

The girls sat down on the living room sofa together. They held hands and tried to help keep a straight face. Ali looked into the phone with her head next to Fleur's. "We love you, Max. Please forgive us."

"Forgive you for what?" he asked.

Ali pulled Fleur's t-shirt up over the baby bump to reveal a fluffy pillow.

Those silly girls. "Are you kidding me? You know, you could give a guy a heart attack with a gag like that. I'm going to hang up now. Too bad too, I had a very nice offer for you."

"Please, Max. We're sorry," Fleur pleaded. "You're just so easy to tease. And we love you. Now, tell us your news."

Max was and will always be a soft touch for the women in his life, so he relented immediately. "I'm taking a trip to India and I may be gone for three or four weeks. Any chance you and Ali would like to come look after the villa for me?"

Fleur caught on quickly. "You said *I'm going*. Where's Lea?"

"Well, that's the thing. I don't know for sure. She and Ingrid went to India together, but only Ingrid came back. I've been advised to go find her if I don't want to lose a wonderful, amazing woman who loves me."

"And who advised you about this?" Fleur asked. "I don't remember getting a call. Did you ask the Guru?"

"No. For once I wanted to leave him out of the equation. But I can guarantee you, it was forces smarter than me."

Ali cracked a smile. "Ha. That leaves the field wide open, Max. Let me huddle with my girl."

Ali and Fleur put their heads together, rubbed noses and kissed. "We accept," Fleur answered. "Give us a couple of days to get things together."

"Excellent!" he replied. "It's settled. I'll leave the key under my favorite Buddha in the garden. Just text me when you have it in your hand. If you can't find it, I'll lead you to it."

"Awesome. Thank you again, so much." Ali's voice matched her smile. "It's perfect timing for us to take a break from here."

"Okay. Great. I have one more question for you. Can I trust you with my scooter?"

"Yes," the girls replied in unison, big smiles on their faces. "Thank you, sweet Max. We're really sorry about the joke."

"No, you're not, but I still love you."

The girls puckered their lips and sent him off with their love and kisses.

Wayan Dharma, one of the new drivers at Om Ham, pulled up in the resort's blue van. He got out to greet Max with the usual Bali smile and happy energy. "Are you ready, Mr. Max?"

"Yep. Packed and ready for adventure. Have you ever been to India, Wayan?"

"No, sir. Travel is not part of my life at this time, but my wife and I always dream about where we will go when the time *is* right."

Wayan looked at the backpack next to Max's feet. "Is that all for you, Mr. Max? Just the backpack?"

"Yes, Wayan. That's it. Light and easy. Let's go."

Wayan picked up the backpack and loaded it into the back of the van as Max jumped in the front seat. Soon they were on the road.

Max looked back towards his villa as they rounded the first curve towards the airport. "Good-bye, Bali. India, here I come."

CHAPTER ELEVEN

India

Max got his boarding passes at the Vietjet Air ticket counter and passed through the security lines with ease. He was familiar and relaxed with the process that so many Bali trips and visa runs prepared him for. He took it all in stride making his way from check point to checkpoint. The last little bit was walking through the seemingly endless duty-free shopping area at the Denpasar airport, known officially as Gusti Ngurah Rai International Airport. Try saying that with a couple of crackers in your mouth.

He looked down at his boarding pass to check the flight times for the tenth time in the last hour. He was calm on the outside, but inside, he was as nervous as a guy riding a level five rapid without a life vest in a rubber raft that was leaking air.

Flight 900 to Hanoi was five hours. There was a two-hour transit time to his second flight, 971, also five hours, into Indira Gandhi International. The passengers in first class were being seated. If he wanted to turn around and go home, he had about fifteen minutes. He didn't. He was ready for this new adventure in spite of all the warnings Master Ketut gave him about what he would see and hear once he started walking the streets of India.

He settled into his economy seat about two rows back from the tail end of the plane, one row from the toilet. He didn't mind. There was a good chance he would need it at some point of the flight, and if the plane were to crash into anything, he was much better off at the rear than right behind the nose. Good to see the bright side of everything.

Lunch service started shortly after takeoff. Max was happy with the meal of tandoori chicken and rice, with a side of lentils and dhal. He loved spicy Indian food in general, so this was a good start to his plan to try as many new Indian foods as possible. Aside from relieving his hunger pains, the plane got a lot quieter. It was a welcome respite. Crowded planes with passengers in close proximity talking non-stop were about as far away from being in the silent cave at Ashram Munivara as humanly possible. Otherwise, he was enjoying the first part of his adventure. He was familiar with Indian people from his days at Om Ham and enjoyed hearing stories about their home and culture.

Max was reading his *Lonely Plant* travel book on India, when he felt a soft tap on his left shoulder. He was in the aisle seat and had not paid much attention to his row mates sitting in the middle and window seats to his left.

"Hello. Is this your first time going to India?"

"Yes. Is it that obvious?"

The beautiful Indian woman in her thirties glanced at his travel book and smiled at him. "India is a big, beautiful country. There is much to see and do. A travel guide is a great start, but if you meet some friendly locals and get invited into someone's home, you will have an experience that is not in any travel guide."

Max loved her accent, and was captivated by her jewelry and tattoos. She had henna tattoos up and down her arms and on her fingers and wrists. There was barely an empty space to tell where her skin began and the tattoos stopped. He was also thankful she decided to break the ice with a little conversation.

"My name is Max. It's so nice to meet you. And who is sitting next to you? Is that your daughter?"

"Hello, Max. My name is Ishani, and this is my daughter, Kavya."

"Ishani. That's a really beautiful name. The names in India are so much more exotic than American names. Does Ishani have a special meaning?"

"Ishani is a Sanskrit name that means Goddess Parvati. It's a popular name in India and it's often used to represent strength and power. Kavya is also a Sanskrit word that means poetry or literature and is often used to represent creativity and intelligence."

"That's a lot of meaning for such a short name. In our early history in America, the Native American Indians often had very meaningful names, but they were much longer, like He Who Runs with the Bears. You didn't have to guess about the meaning with those names."

Kavya giggled. "That's funny. But your American names also have meaning, don't they?

Kavya's question brought out the teacher in Max. He loved teaching. "Yes, they do. For sure. But the meanings were far more practical. Like in the old days before America was getting settled and families immigrated from Europe, if a father was a baker, it was not unusual for his last name to be Baker. If the father was a blacksmith, his last name was Smith."

Kavya enjoyed listening to Max. "What about your name, Mr. Max?"

"Ahh, my last name was Rabinowitz before it was changed, and my family was a family of Rabbis."

"Your names fit so perfectly, it seems," Kavya replied.

"I guess it made sense a long while ago. But they sure don't have the beauty of your name and your mom's."

"Thank you, Max. That is kind of you to say."

"Well, if I'm not being too nosy or too personal, do you mind if I ask about all the art on your arms and fingers? And on your daughter as well?"

"Not at all. In India, art is displayed everywhere, including on our bodies. Tattoos are part of the art in our culture. They can represent so many different aspects of a family or individual, from wealth and cast to profession and ideology."

Max was taken in by the women and was listening with a captivated mind and heart.

Ishani continued. "Henna is mainly used in celebration of special occasions such as weddings and birthdays in the joyous gathering of people. The Henna paste symbolizes good health and prosperity in marriage, and in some cultures, the darker the henna stain, the deeper the love between two individuals."

"Thank you. I'm so excited to land in India now. Can an American get a henna tattoo?"

"Of course. You will see many street artists sitting with their supplies ready to offer you a sample of our culture. And remember, the location of the tattoos is also meaningful."

"Like what?" Max asked.

"Well, for one, the feet are truly a spiritual place for henna, as they connect the body, mind and spirit with the earth."

"It's all so interesting to me. So many of my friends have been to India. Some many years ago to follow their yogis or gurus, and others to simply learn about your country and way of life. I can't believe I'm finally going to see for myself."

Ishani was happy to talk to Max. He expressed a real and genuine interest in her and her daughter, and she could feel his open heart the moment they were all seated for their flight. "It's never too late to visit the most beautiful and spiritual place in the world, Max. What finally prompted your visit to India?"

Max was more than impressed with Ishani's command of the English language and her openness to talk about real things in life. "Love," he replied after just a moment's hesitation.

Ishani smiled. Kavya perked up and looked at Max. She was such a beautiful young woman. Her dark eyes and smooth as silk skin were second only to her incredible smile. "Are you in love with an India girl?" she asked.

Max laughed gently at this beautiful young girl's injection into their conversation. She was uninhibited and also spoke perfect English. Before Max could answer, Ishani looked back at her daughter. "Kavya, be respectful. That's a personal question."

"Yes, Mom. I'm sorry." Then the sweet young girl looked at Max and said, "I'm sorry Max."

"It's okay. It's a very reasonable question. I am in love, but my girlfriend is from Perth, Australia."

"And she's in India now?" the little girl, who was probably twelve or thirteen asked.

"Yes. Good guess. At least I hope that's where she is. I want to surprise her and tell her how much I love her."

"That's very romantic," Kavya replied. This little girl was wise beyond her years and obviously into romance. India makes more movies each year than Hollywood, and their studios were given the nickname Bollywood. So, was only natural for a thirteen-year-old girl to ask about love and marriage when the young population was used to movies filled with love stories that featured romance, songs and huge wedding parties.

The flight attendants came down the rows to pick up the lunch trays. Max, Ishani and the irrepressible Kavya settled back in their seats. Their conversation went back and forth, and by the time the captain announced the plane would be landing in Not Bai

International Airport in Hanoi in twenty minutes, Max felt like he made two new friends.

Ishani's family lived in Kathmandu, the capital of Nepal, and they would be taking a different connecting flight than Max. They were on an adventure of their own, stopping in Hanoi for a few days before heading home. He was sad to see them go. It was nice to have someone to talk to while he figured out where the heck he was and how he was going to get there.

Kathmandu was also high on his list of things to do other than finding Lea. When they all reached the transit area, they shook hands and traded contact information on their phones and wished each other a happy trip. Ishani was so kind, she insisted Max find the time to visit her in Kathmandu, with Lea or on his own. However, things worked out. Kavya, of course, just wanted to know if she could come to the wedding if it was in India.

Max was happy to be in the airport as strange as it was to him. It seemed like it took forever to get off the plane, and by the time he made it to the Hanoi airport food court, he was hungry. On the plane, he read that pho, a Vietnamese soup made with broth, rice noodles, herbs and either meat or tofu was the number one local food to try. Number two, was bun cha, a dish which includes vermicelli, grilled pork, vegetables and dipping sauce with pickled papaya and carrot. He had never been to Vietnam and was excited to at least get a small taste of another country, even it was just a couple of hours at the airport.

He stopped under a sign that read **BIG BOWL**. He studied the menu and finally decided on the bun cha and a large green tea. He found a table near the flight boards and sat down. How could he go wrong with a restaurant called Big Bowl?!

CHAPTER TWELVE

New Delhi

Max found his seat quickly for this last leg of this part of the adventure. The full day of travel finally hit him. He was asleep just moments after takeoff and was in such a deep sleep, the next thing he was aware of, was the captain's voice announcing their arrival time, weather, and connecting flight instructions.

"I can't believe it," he proclaimed out loud. A few of the passengers deplaning around him turned to see who he was talking to, but he didn't care. He just smiled at them. He was landing in New Delhi, India.

He felt a little uneasy, and wasn't quite sure if it was his lunch from the Big Bowl in the Hanoi airport, or that his quest for finding Lea was about to begin. He settled on it being a combination of the two, but just to be sure, he decided he would stick to fruit and bottled water for a little while.

Customs and immigration went smoothly. He was happy he had only his backpack. The passengers waiting for luggage would find a much longer line waiting for them at the passport station. He declared his Sumatran coffee from Bali, had his backpack scanned by two stiff looking security agents, and finally made the last turn leading to the exit of the Indira Gandhi International Airport.

The airport itself was dirty. Not at all like the photos he saw in the few YouTube videos he checked out before his trip. The arrival hall, which is something he had a little experience with in Malaysia, was huge. It had an open layout with tiled floors and people moving everywhere. He knew New Delhi was one of the biggest hubs in India, but he didn't expect it to be so old and ramshackle looking. There was basically nowhere to sit, but even amongst the mayhem, he could smell some really delicious food from the cafes he walked past. Food would have to wait. He wanted to get to his hotel and figure the rest out from there.

He was finally standing outside in India. He was never so happy to actually *see* and *smell* air. The smog was so heavy, that cars and taxis just a few yards from his exit at baggage claim were hardly visible. *Not even the worst day in Los Angeles was is bad. I'll have to remember this the next time I'm about to complain about California smog.*

And so, here it was. His first step out of the airport would be one he would never forget. He inhaled deeply. Everything he had heard and read came to life in that first big inhale. He let it out slowly. Now all he had to do was find a taxi If he could make out the outline of a car through the brown haze that engulfed everything.

He looked out at the travel options. There were cars, buses, motorcycles, auto rickshaws, and cycle-rickshaws all standing at the ready. But, with the heat and humidity at mid-day highs, he decided on a regular gas driven taxi with a driver. He would leave the more adventurous get around choices for later.

He studied the listings on Booking dot com before he left Bali, and decided on Hotel Blue Pearl. The photos were impressive and it was a highly rated hotel with breakfast included. The total for two days was $66. He wasn't trying to be cheap, but from the hotels he checked out, Blue Pearl was higher quality than many others. He hoped the price included a bed, and hot water would be greatly appreciated.

He smiled wondering to himself. *Why am I being so hard on India?* He couldn't help himself, but he was very aware that there were $5,000-a-night hotels ready and available for the elites of the world. *I'm sorry, India,* he thought, still smiling.

The hotel was only six miles from the airport and the New Delhi Train Station was only half a mile. He booked two days for a couple of reasons. For one, he would have time to take a short train ride just for the experience, and secondly, he could rest, talk to the hotel office about his options for getting to Rishikesh, and then make his best decision.

The taxi ride was easy, even if the air-conditioning came in the form of roll down windows. It was perfect. He sat next to the window and took in as much as he could. The view, not the air. It was odd to see cows walking the streets with the same sense of purpose as the many sadhus or holy men. There were cows stopped at shanty's or businesses for a bit of grass that was growing up the cracks in the sidewalks, or a sip of water if the pot hole was deep enough.

Bali dogs had prepared him for this in some ways, in that they are not fed very often and are usually bone thin with splotchy skin. It looked like the cows suffered the same fate here in India. He didn't enjoy seeing emaciated animals of any kind.

Donovan, his good friend from Om Ham, suggested he find a driver to get to Rishikesh to really see the countryside. It was an interesting thought, but the drive was eight hours. Compare that to the flight, which was listed at 55 minutes, and it seemed like a no brainer, as they say.

What he saw on the short ride from the airport to the hotel might have to suffice. Samir, his taxi driver, asked him the usual questions about where he was from, how long he would be in New Delhi, and if he could help in any way. He instantly reminded Max of a regular day in Bali. In Ubud, the first question any taxi driver asked when the ride started, after asking for your name, was "How long you stay?" After more than a few rides trying to explain his itinerary, he finally learned to say he was leaving the next morning. It made life much easier. The drivers were just trying to make a buck, but it's not like taxis are hard to come by.

He laughed to himself when his mind replayed the familiar Ubud refrain the taxi drivers would shout out as tourists walked by… "Taxi, Mister? Taxi, Mister?" They would shout at you from a block away until you were out of sight. So, when Samir asked, he explained he was only there two nights. In this case it was true, and he hoped that would put an end to questions about his plans in India.

Samir was not one to give up easily. "So, where you go after two days? I can go anywhere."

Max laughed in his friendly manner. "All right, Samir. I was thinking of going up North."

Samir beamed with enthusiasm. "There are so many beautiful sights in India that will take your breath away. Where up north? I give you very good rate."

"Rishikesh," Max replied.

"The flight is so short. I don't know if I want to be in a car for eight hours."

Samir drove and talked about the long drive, the beautiful scenery and friendly people in the villages.

Max listened while he thought about the possibilities and the suggestion of his good friend Donovan. Donovan lived in India for a few years while getting his yoga teacher certification, and it was always worth taking his ideas into consideration. Max valued his input on spiritual matters at Om Ham, and he knew Donovan would lead him on a productive and informative journey in India if he would allow himself to be as adventurous as his friend.

Mention of going North, seemed of great interest to Samir. Like any taxi or tour driver in Bali, he was always on the lookout for a way to earn money and it is widely known Americans can be generous tippers. With five children and a handful of goats to feed, any opportunity for a big payday was worth checking out.

"Let me think about it, Samir. How's this? Take me to a great restaurant tonight and join me for dinner. We will have a good meal and talk about it."

"Very well, Mr. Max. I pick you up at eight and I will take you someplace very special. Tell me where you are going and I will explore the best roads for a safe journey."

"Parmarth Niketan Ashram to be specific. Do you know the place?"

"Yes, Mr. Max. It is a well-known yoga institution. I have been there many times to drop off Westerners on their spiritual path."

Samir's 2012 Mercedes Diesel pulled up in front of the Blue Pearl Hotel, sputtering just a bit, as smoke billowed out of the tail pipes. He opened the door for Max to get out and grabbed his backpack from the trunk. Max looked at the sputtering car with a quizzical look.

"Not to worry, Mr. Max. Once we are on the main roads, we will have a smooth ride and no smoke. Trust me. See you at eight." Max pulled a few bills from his pocket and handed Samir three one hundred-rupee notes (about two dollars and fifty cents American value) as a tip. He wasn't sure if that was a good tip or not, but he would know for sure if Samir showed up at the hotel at eight for their dinner date.

It was only a matter of minutes before some of Max's fears about wandering around India presented themselves. As soon as Samir left and he was standing alone with his bags, he noticed people hanging around the fringes of the hotel. They walked slowly in his direction with an almost zombie like expression on their faces as they approached.

Once in front of him, they begged for his attention to buy something or go see a friend of theirs to buy something or get a ride somewhere or other services. It was unrelenting and unnerving. It was much like the streets of Ubud, Bali near the markets and businesses in town, but the similarity was not reassuring. In Ubud, he would often put some cash or coins into the open hands of young mothers sitting with little babies still suckling at their bosom.

He felt bad for anyone struggling to survive on the streets, and once Bali and its people were familiar to him, he was able to smile and offer whatever he had in his pockets. It felt good and the people always offered a blessing of thanks. Maybe India would feel that way in time, but for the beginning of his journey and all the questions it held, all he could do in this present moment was to look past the hopeless faces in front of him and enter the hotel lobby.

Thankfully, inside the hotel was a much different scene. It was quiet and the air was cool from the wall mounted air conditioning units. A beautiful young Indian woman, Neha according to her name tag, welcomed him and led him to the registration desk. There, a tall uniformed desk clerk, Aarush, welcomed him officially to the Blue Pearl. He scanned his passport, ordered a welcome drink to his room, and sent him on his way with an old-fashioned key you had to actually put in the door to open.

It was already seven. Max took a quick shower, put on a clean shirt and shorts, and went down to the lobby to wait for Samir.

Samir showed up right at eight and in just a few minutes his car stopped at what looked on first sight, as a very nice restaurant. The sign out front said Delhi Ka Tadka. As soon as they entered, Max was happy with Samir's choice. He was impressed. The ambiance was beautiful, and from what he could glean from the plates of food being placed on the tables around him, the Indian food of New Delhi looked delicious, fresh, and right out of the oven or off the grill.

The aroma of all the foods and spices instantly reminded him of one his favorite Indian restaurants in Los Angeles, Star of India. The array of colors was as bright as the costumes at an Indian wedding.

Max went with a safe choice of Tandoori Chicken while Samir had a more local dish of Chicken Tikka masala. It was marinated chicken chunks in a spiced sauce of yogurt, cream, tomato, onion garlic and ginger. Samir added his own pinch of chili peppers for a little extra punch.

The aroma was intoxicating. Max dove into his meal with gusto. He dipped his naan bread into the sauce and juices from his chicken and veggies and in barely a few minutes, his plate was clean.

"I will guess you enjoyed your meal, Mr. Max."

"Yes, Samir. Thank you. It was delicious."

Samir took a folded paper from his jacket pocket and laid it on the table. "This is the best route to Rishikesh. It will take almost eight hours and that will include a few stops I believe you will enjoy to see. We will go through many small villages and if you like, we can stop and talk to families and shop owners. They are very curious about Americans and may want to take your picture or at the very least ask you questions. Do you like?"

"I will think about it and call you in the morning, I promise. Tomorrow I am going to take a short train ride just for the experience. Thank you, Samir. It was a great first day in India."

Samir bowed politely and he and Max shook hands good night. Max asked if he could take a selfie with him before he left. Samir obliged and Max had his first photo from India. One of him and his smiling taxi driver.

The day started in Bali and was ending in India. It passed quickly and Max was happy to have hot running water and an assortment of teas waiting for him on the bedside table. He learned a lot in 24 hours, and was thinking he might change his mind and take the longer scenic route to Rishikesh.

He was tired and sore, and forced himself to do some stretching on the floor followed by a sleep-inducing meditation to ease himself into some good dreams. Lucid dreams if he was lucky. Morning would come soon enough and he felt he accomplished a lot for his first day in India. Tomorrow would be thoughts of getting to Rishikesh and finding Lea.

CHAPTER THIRTEEN

Ingrid

To Ingrid, the sun was an aphrodisiac. She was in heaven being able to use Max's Villa while he was away. Her place in Ubud, a little south of the Monkey Forest, was nice, but quite spartan compared to the beautiful villa Max and Lea often invited her to for meals or tea or just a hang out in the garden. Max messaged her on WhatsApp to say Fleur and Ali were on their way, and to please keep everything clean and ready. "

All right," she said to herself and the songbirds in the garden. It was just her, the always magical white herons, and the butterflies. "I may as well enjoy it while I have it to myself." With that in mind, Ingrid opened the French doors wide and turned on the jets for the jacuzzi.

She pushed down on her yoga pants and slid her long legs over the edge of the spa. She wasn't wearing anything else. She was a simple girl in that sense. Commando all the way, unless she was going dancing in town or had a date with someone she wanted to see her lacy, girlie things. She reached behind her and pulled up on her T-shirt until it was over her head and off. She used it as a towel and placed it on the ledge so she could lie flat and have a little protection from the hot tiles beneath her.

The sun's rays were already working their magic. She was enjoying the heat and the tingling sensations her body was feeling from top to bottom. She brought her feet flat on the edge of the pool with her knees up and her back flat. She opened and closed them, moving them wide apart and closing them together in a rapid motion.

Then, she put her knees together, and moved them down to the ground in each direction. First left, then right, always exhaling to the right, just as she was taught. It was a trance like mudra of sex and yoga that with focus and repetition would be sure to activate the kundalini energy center at the base of the spine. From there, with effort and concentration, the energy would move up to the crown chakra and out.

Healing and pleasure at the same time was Kundalini Tantra at its finest. And not that she needed any proof, but her t-shirt towel was already soaked with the pheromones of her enviable sensuality. She lifted her small butt up as high as she could, held the position for a deep breath, then exhaled and came down. She reached forward to grab her ankles, helping to arch her back as high as possible. Wash, rinse, repeat. Eleven times was the minimum to get the desired effect. Master Ketut endorsed this pose for keeping the hips open and the sacral chakra clear. He would be proud.

She shifted her position into standing tall for a few sun salutations. She lifted her arms high above her head with her palms touching each other over her crown chakra, took a deep breath in, held it, then exhaled slowly and loudly through the mouth as she lowered her arms to the ground, with her hands wrapped behind her ankles.

She leaned forward as far as she could, pulled her chest to her knees. She then inhaled, bringing her arms back up over her head, and exhaled as she arched backwards from the waist as her head fell back and her eyes looked up at the clouds. She stretched fully with her palms still touching, pointing behind her.

To finish the set, she brought her arms together over her head, then lowered them slowly to prayer pose as she exhaled. At this point, Ingrid was in an elevated state of consciousness.

She dropped carefully to her little *towel,* and rested her head on a small pillow from one of the lawn chairs. Her legs were straight forward with her hands to her side, palms up. She inhaled deeply, inhaling the energy and aromas she was engulfed in. It was like she was on auto-pilot. Her knees came up with her heels flat on the tiles. They drifted apart naturally, allowing the cool pre-thunderstorm breeze to wash over her while creating a slight opening for a different kind of sensation.

Her right hand found its way down over her smooth mound and between her thighs. Her fingers disappeared into her sex, her body moving in its own rhythm. She was so intoxicated, she might not have cared if she was in a yoga class with others or, like now, alone at the spa. As life will be sometimes, even if she wasn't thinking about testing that hypothesis, the universe had other ideas.

Ali and Fleur watched in silence. They only briefly looked at each other before turning back to Ingrid. They reached for each other's hands without looking away. The moment their fingers touched, they interlocked and stood shoulder to shoulder. Their fingers moved, caressing each other as they watched. They each felt a different sense of awe in the way Ingrid's body moved with such graceful sexuality. She was beautiful, taut, and flexible as a yoga ninja.

They were only there a moment, but the vision made a lasting impression. They weren't embarrassed at their inability to look away. No one would be. It was *that* beautiful to see. They looked at each other again, unsure if they should slink back inside to make a loud noise so Ingrid would know she was no longer alone, or just say something.

They were saved from making a choice when Ingrid swiveled her head toward them. "Hi, girls. I was expecting you. Not today though, or I would have prepared a more appropriate reception."

"We're so sorry," Ali said.

"You're a goddess," Fleur added, her face still a bit red from the natural state of blushing she experienced. "Please excuse our incredibly lousy timing. We were able to get a flight out the night Max called, so we just went for it."

Ingrid was more at ease than one might expect at such an intimate and private moment. It's possible she enjoyed the audience. "It's fine," she said as she stood up and pulled her yoga pants back on. "This is your home and I hope you have a happy and wonderful time while you're here. Let me get my things together. If you would hand me my big beach bag just inside the door, I have a top in there."

"You know, don't have to leave right now," Ali said.

"Your yoga asanas are beautiful. I would like to be able to do what you just did," Fleur added. "Most of it, anyway," she said laughing. Fleur walked back to the French doors to grab Ingrid's beach tote.

"I'm happy to show you both a few poses on another day. I have to get going to my batik class today though. Yoga is a really great way to nurture and pamper yourself."

"That would be great," Fleur said. "I can use all the help I can get."

Ali was equally enthralled with Ingrid's presence. Her gaze was still firmly on her tan, partially unclothed body. "And please, come by for dinner in a couple of days. We would love to have you over and talk to you about Bali and what's going on with Max and Lea. That is if you don't mind sharing the latest gossip. We were both surprised."

Fleur handed Ingrid her bag. Even in the simple act of putting her top on, Ingrid was sensuality in motion. "Thank you. Remember, there's no need for clothes around here, as you can see. Enjoy yourselves. It's heaven on earth. I would love to join you for dinner. Just let me know the day. Max told me how close you all are and it would be nice to get to know you."

"Excuse me, where's the bathroom I gotta pee," Fleur, who was not much for subtlety, said.

"First door on the right, into the master bath. Make yourself at home." Ingrid was being as cordial as possible, even though she had hoped for at least a few more days to herself.

Fleur dashed off. Ali was struck by Ingrid's beauty and was not shy about it. "Give me your phone. I'll add my number, if that's all right." Ali had a seductive smile on her lips as she took Ingrid's phone and added her contact. "Here you go. Call anytime."

Ingrid seemed equally interested in Ali. She had that certain *je ne sais quoi*, even though it was Fleur who was from Paris. She was an unconventional woman and if there was an attraction she wanted to explore with either men or women, her spirit was free to all possibilities. In this case however, she might not have realized the door she was opening could come with consequences she never would have anticipated.

Fleur turned the corner into the garden and saw Ali hand Ingrid her phone. She didn't say anything. Ali didn't see her come back in, and for now, it seemed to Fleur like a secret worth holding onto. Harmless or not.

"Did I hear someone say something about yoga for two?" Fleur said in a cheerful and genuine tone. Her presence until that moment had been completely undetected.

Ingrid grabbed an apple from the fruit basket in the kitchen on her way out, and said, "Thanks again for the invite, girls. I hope to see you both soon. Ciao."

"Ciao!" Fleur shouted back.

When she heard the door close, she looked at Ali who had started to unpack in their temporary bedroom. "So, what do you think of Ingrid?"

"She seems nice," Ali replied.

"Is that all?" Fleur asked.

Ali raised her eyebrows a bit as she asked, "What do you mean? Do you have a problem with something?"

"No," Fleur answered. "She's very sexy. I thought you noticed."

Ali detected a little jealousy in Fleur's comments. Something she didn't want to get into, but seemed to be popping up lately in similar situations in L.A. Instead, she said, "The way you grabbed my hand when we were watching her, it felt like you noticed something. *N'est pas?*"

Fleur was too tired for a bit of sarcasm from Ali, and in French no less. She dished it back. *"Je prends l'autre chambre. Bon soir."* *Let her look it up,* she said to herself.

CHAPTER FOURTEEN
Sadar Bazaar

Max woke up feeling energized. After looking over his Lonely Planet travel guide for India, he chose to spend a few hours at one of the most popular markets/bazars in this part of India, the Sadar Bazaar. It was listed as a prime shopping destination, including items from electronics and clothing, to spices and imitation jewelry, and much more. Too much to list, the travel guide said. And he figured, if he did find Lea, it couldn't hurt to have a little jewelry in his pocket. Imitation or not.

The small breakfast area at the Blue Pearl Hotel was buzzing with guests picking at the ornately decorated buffet table. The over filled trays of food all looked delicious, and in a tip of the hat to all the American and European guests, the Indian labels of what was being served had corresponding descriptions in English. Of course, eggs still looked like eggs regardless of the language, so for Max, it was time to dig in and get the day started.

After working his way down the row of hot and cold entrees, he found the one dish he had heard so much about. Chole bhature. It's a combination of chana masala (spicy white chickpeas) and bhatura/ puri, a deep-fried bread made from maida, an all-purpose Indian flour. It's mostly a Northern India dish, but he was happy it was right here in front of him.

This dish was served at Indian restaurants all over Los Angeles, but he'd never tried it. Now, he could have the real thing. He could always fast for a day or two once he returned to Bali, or like Julia Roberts in *Eat, Pray, Love,* just buy bigger pants.

He loved breakfast, so he dug in. He scooped up a large portion, then moved to the tray of scrambled eggs that were sprinkled with something orange, and thankfully, it was turmeric and not some hot Indian spice. There was a big plate of aloo paratha, which is unleavened bread stuffed with a spiced mixture of mashed potatoes. And next to that was a huge tray mixed with rice, smoked pork, and steamed vegetables.

It all looked good and the only true danger was over eating. He took small spoonsful of each tray to fill his plate, saving the last bit of room for the khura, a pancake made with buckwheat flour. He would have loved his morning Sumatran Latte' to help wash it all down, but, when in India… Tea was the morning hot drink here, and his favored oat milk was replaced with a butter tea made of yak milk. One sip was all he could handle. One more might cause him to yak the yak so to speak. There had to be a Starbucks somewhere, right?

Max looked down at his stomach, as if that would tell him how this wild mixture of food was going to settle. He decided he would be fine, and asked the front desk to get him a rickshaw cycle to the train station. Today would be a day of new experiences.

Aarush, the all-purpose concierge of the hotel, arranged a rickshaw cycle for Max at eight A.M. He was out front of the hotel to begin his adventure. He decided on his black Venice Beach board shorts and a white Santa Monica California long-sleeved t-shirt with surfboards imprinted on the back. *It's not like I'm going to be mistaken for a local by wearing a turban,* he thought. He wore similar outfits in Bali with great success.

In fact, as he liked to point out to friends who mocked his wardrobe, one day at his favorite Bali restaurant, Zest, a beautiful young woman in her San Diego Chargers tank top came up to him and said she loved what he was wearing. He was surprised, and taken in by her beautiful eyes, long dark curly hair and bright smile. Still, he managed to say, "Thank you."

She'd responded with, "No problem dude. You gotta represent."

He'd laughed and smiled. Young kids. So free and at peace with a language all their own. In L.A. if he looked too long at a beautiful young woman, he'd be called something else — the term sketchy is popular these days.

In Bali, the younger Gen Z and every other generation were mostly seeking a better life, a happier life, in a different way. In Bali, there were no corporate ladders to climb, only a chart to mark your progress on the yoga mat. Life was not that way in Los Angeles. Max loved his Bali and he hoped India would prove to be the same.

A broken-down cycle rickshaw with a partially ripped back seat pulled up and the driver waved at him. He appeared to be in his sixties or seventies with a long white beard and patches of hair on his head. He pulled up to Max, and with a broad toothless smile asked, "Train station? Come. We go."

Max pushed his desire to decline out of his mind and sat in the back of the rickshaw. The ride to the New Delhi Railway Station was short, and even though the amount of smoke he inhaled on the way was equal to a pack of cigarettes, he felt good.

The New Delhi Railway Station glistened under the morning sun. It looked modern and accessible from the outside. Max was happy to be out of the rickshaw without any splinters in his ass and excited to experience another first in India. He joined the crowd of people standing in line at a ticket kiosk.

He scanned the long list of departures and station stops as he plucked his trusty Visa card from his wallet. Sure enough, there was a sign marking the stop for the Bazaar. It was only a 30-minute ride with two stops.

He walked from the Kiosk to the huge layout of trains and tracks. Before he needed to go left or right, he noticed he was standing on platform eleven. Seven minutes for the next train to Sadar Bazaar. He was on the right track. Literally.

Once inside the train, he was face to face with a mass of humanity. It didn't matter which car he entered, they were all the same. Seats filled and the aisles clogged with strap holders. There were men in suits, briefcases at their side ready for a meeting or a day at the office.

There were also men and women dressed in rags clutching their purses or snacks as if their life depended on it. Maybe it did. Max had been on many trains in his life, from Italy to France and even Australia. Nothing compared to this. It was the train version of the movie scene many of us think of showing poor people and young travelers riding on old buses up steep hills in Peru or other such places, with passengers holding onto their cats, chickens, or goats.

Max scanned the car for a seat. One stood out, mainly because it was the only one left. It was an aisle seat next to what he guessed was a Holy man. The man's clothing was an orange colored robe with a matching cloth turban folded and wrapped perfectly on top of his head.

The man had a full beard that despite looking like it was growing in all directions with a life of its own, looked regal in its natural colors of black, gray and a speckled mixture of both. It went far down past his chin getting wider towards its end point near the bottom of his neck. He wore a beautiful religious or spiritual pendant around his neck as well as an amulet with a tassel at the end where the beads or crystals are separated by a larger stone. He sat tall. His piercing dark eyes and dark smooth skin highlighted an absolute aura of calmness.

Max was familiar with amulets. He had a few of his own and thought about adding to his collection while in India. A prayer amulet is one hundred and eight beads that are used in Hindu prayers or meditations such as Om Nama Shiva Ya. The proper meditation is to say those words while rolling the larger bead between your thumb and middle finger as you chant the mantra. When you get to the big bead at the center, you have said the mantra one hundred and eight times. If this practice is done three times, it is considered the perfect meditation to still the mind.

Max stopped at the open seat. He lowered his head gently and asked quietly, "May I join you?" He kind of sat as he asked, hoping for the holy man's approval.

"Yes, by all means. It would be silly for you to stand here leaning."

Max smiled and nodded his head as he lowered himself to the seat. The man's English was better than his. Probably his vocabulary as well.

"Thank you." Max felt comfortable and at ease. It wasn't as if the train were filled with young hooligans like the famous Chicago EL trains. He was glad those days were long over. All you had to do was miss a stop by a few city blocks, and if you got off the wrong platform, danger lurked. Whenever he was on those city trains, he would sit next to a cop or a priest when possible. Not here though. This was good.

When he exhaled loudly, involuntarily, the holy man said, "You know how to breathe to let out the chi. That will serve you well in life wherever you are."

Max realized he'd been louder than he meant to be. "I'm sorry. It's kind of automatic with me. It helps me relax."

"Your first time in India I take it? Where are you going?"

"Yes. I arrived yesterday and today, I'm going to the Sadar Bazaar. It looks like an amazing place to visit."

"It is an institution, as you say in your country. Be careful. There are pickpockets everywhere, and most of them are under ten years old and you won't even see them."

"Good to know," he replied. "My name is Max. It's so nice to meet you."

"My name is Vikram. Nice to meet you as well. I live with my family in Saket, not too far from your stop for the Bazaar. Maybe just another ten kilometers. Do you plan to visit our famous city of Nepal and see the Taj Mahal?"

"Maybe not on this trip. I'm actually going to Rishikesh tomorrow to the Parmarth Niketan Ashram."

For once, Max didn't want to talk about his trip. His interest was in the Holy Man. "I don't mean to be nosey, but are you a holy man? I couldn't help but notice your robe and amulets. It's kind of why I sat down next to you."

"That and there were no other seats, right?"

Vikram was funny and sharp as a tack as Americans say. "Busted. You're right. But I also go to holy temples in Bali and practice many Hindu chants during ceremonies and yoga classes. I would love to hear about your spiritual interests, if I'm not being rude and you don't mind sharing."

"Not rude at all, Max. There are many holy men in India from Sadhus, Yogis, Rishi, and many other forms of service or learning. I am from a family of Brahmins. Do you know of us?"

"That's an upper-class caste, right? I had a yoga teacher in California who came from a wealthy Brahmin family. He was taught kundalini yoga by special masters who were only available to very wealthy people."

"I have heard of Yogi Bhajan from India who brought kundalini yoga to the West. Is this of who you speak?"

"Yes. Wow. I'm surprised you know of him. From what I understood, he was more popular in America than here in India."

"The world is a small place, Max. Even here in India."

"I heard many stories about him, but there was one in particular that I'll never forget."

"Tell me, Max. It will be interesting to learn if I have also heard the story."

"All right. But stop me if I start to ramble. Anyway, we were told in class that before Yogi Bhajan left for the west, he was warned by his masters that if he taught the secrets of kundalini yoga to the West, he would be dead within a year. Nine months after he arrived in California, he fell into a coma. A dozen of his disciples and proteges gathered at his hospital room and chanted for hours and he came out of the coma."

"That's quite a story. But, I can believe it. Just like in Bali and Thailand, it is also true for India that the dark and light side of life must coexist. The power of prayer and mantras can do harm or good. Thank you for sharing that story. I think it was meant for you to experience Yogi Bhajan as your teacher."

"Thank you, Vikram. I would like to learn about your spiritual practice and see the temples where you study."

"Well, Max, if you want to check out the bazaar another day, you are welcome to come with me to my home. My wife will cook us a great feast and you will meet my two beautiful daughters, Savitri and Rhada."

"I would love to. Is it far? I left all my things in my room at the hotel."

"Not to worry, Max. I will have my driver take you back first thing in the morning. You can enjoy a traditional home-cooked meal and see the sights on your way back to the hotel. I can even have him drop you at the Bazaar. It is open very early. Come, you will be my guest for the night."

Max leaned back in his seat. He felt a tingling sensation that something special was happening. He felt like he was receiving a blessing from a holy man on his first train ride in India. "Thank you, God."

CHAPTER FIFTEEN

At the Home of a Holy Man

Devi Patel, tall and well built, stood at the driver's side door of a shiny new black and silver Mercedes-Maybach S600. He was dressed in a coffee colored suit with three black stripes on each arm just above the wrist. His hands were covered by white gloves and he wore an airplane captain's style hat with the bill reaching out over his forehead. He proudly held the door open once he noticed his boss approach with his guest.

"Welcome back, sir. Did you have a good trip?"

"Yes, Devi. Thank you. It was wonderful to see my sister and her family after such a long time."

"It's only been three days, sir."

"And to me, a lifetime, my friend. Devi, this is my guest, Max, from America by way of Bali."

Devi held out his had to shake. "Welcome. It is a pleasure to meet you. Will you be joining us at the master's house?"

Vikram stepped in to answer. "Yes, Devi. And please, take the scenic route so our guest can see what a beautiful city New Delhi is."

"Yes, sir. With great pleasure."

Max and Vikram got in the back seat of the ultra-cool luxury car. Devi closed the passenger doors for them and got behind the wheel. He accelerated gracefully, handling the V6 diesel powered limousine with ease. The car was smooth and quiet. When the doors closed, the rest of the world was shut off to everyone inside. The air-conditioning was perfectly cool, and Indian music played softly through all sixteen speakers. Chilled water bottles, assorted juices and snacks were within reach.

"This is really spectacular." Max beamed. "I can't thank you enough. It's not at all what I expected."

"Everything happens for a reason, Max. Do you believe in this principle?"

"Very much. Sometimes the reason is more obvious than others and circumstances are so much different. I can't even imagine what could come of something so unexpected."

"Don't think about what you can't predict. Enjoy where you are, who you're with, and what you are doing. There is an old Indian saying to bring good fortune into your life, be thankful for all you have and excited about all that is on the way."

Max could not wipe the smile off his face. "I like that saying. It's similar to morning affirmations I have learned about, but I'm still blown away. I usually get around on a scooter. It's really fun to be in such a luxurious car."

Vikram smiled and took his new friend's hands in his. "We are here on this earth to love each other and make use of our time. This is a Vedic and Hindu philosophy. It's a blessing for me and my family to bring you into our home. If you're here long enough, you will find that the people of India are so happy to share their life, their good fortune, and their time to give to others. It's part of our spirituality. It's why people come to India from all over the world to find what is missing in their life at home, wherever that is."

Max's eyes focused on the scenery surrounding him in every direction—mountains in the distance, verdant hillsides everywhere. People and cows sharing the road just as he had seen in the YouTube videos he studied before his trip.

More than once, Devi had to dodge a cart being pulled by oxen. At a stop sign, there was an old woman lying on the side of the road. Her wrinkled skin and leathery face revealed a life of pain and suffering. It was a life far different than the one his host was taking him to. He put his head down and brought his hands up brushing through his hair trying to make sense of it all and get it out of his mind all at the same time.

Max's reaction to this poor woman did not escape Vikram.

Vikram was a deep thinker and offered his thoughts freely. "Closing your eyes and pretending to not see the poor and unfortunate does not make them go away," he said in an almost fatherly way. "In fact, they offer us all a chance to be better human beings."

Max let out a deep breath again. A long one. "It's so hard for me to see the pain of others right in front of me while I have been blessed with so much abundance in my life. It doesn't make sense sometimes. I think of myself as a good person, a helpful and loving person, but I don't know what I did to deserve all that I have."

"I can feel the goodness in you, Max, so you must allow yourself to receive the abundance God has put in front of you. When you feel worthy of all that comes into your life, more will come. That is the true law of attraction and the law of the universe."

"Being a student of yoga and a practitioner of meditation and chanting, have you heard of Dharma?" Max was eager to get into a spiritual conversation and a little bit of his ego wanted to let this holy man from New Delhi know he had some understanding of life outside of the physical realm.

"I have. It means path, right?"

"Yes. Path is surely a part of the bigger picture. Dharma is a Sanskrit word and has more than one meaning. We can say there is a cosmic law, Dharma of the universe. In English, it can be translated to mean nature.

In this case we are talking about the nature of beings. It can be a person's nature to teach, to build great buildings, to be an artist who inspires generations of people. So, we can always ask ourselves, what is our true dharma, our true nature. In terms of humanity, dharma is to awaken, to raise our conscious mind to create a world that is in harmony."

"So, where does karma come into all this?"

"Good question, Max. Karma is what we are left with when we are consumed with a world view of right and wrong. Karma comes from the worst of where our ego takes us. It is not about awakening to our higher selves. It's about reliving all that has hurt us in our lives. It is the people who fall into the same bad relationships over and over again, making the same bad choices in any aspect of life. Not just in relationships."

"But there is good karma as well, right?"

"Of course, Max. There has to be. It is like another old saying, 'do one good deed and ten come back to you.'"

"The circle of life," Max added.

Max was so taken by the wisdom of his host, he didn't even notice the car stopped in front of a magnificent estate. Devi's voice brought him into the present moment. "Shall I pull into the garage, sir or are you going out later?"

"Let's park it for the night, Devi. It will be dark soon and I know our guest will be full from an amazing meal and too satisfied to want to get up."

"Yes, sir. Vanya is an exceptional cook. I will drop you at the front door, then park."

Max had to laugh at that thought. To be dropped off at the front door so the car could be driven to the garage. Sure enough, there was room for three decent-sized villas in the space between the garage and the house. And the space was filled with designer landscaping of sculptures, fountains, and magnificent palm trees.

Max stepped out on the left side of the car and could not believe his eyes. He was standing in front of a gorgeous stone washed white home, two stories with a stunning deck on the second floor and gorgeous windows all around. There was a marble entryway leading to three steps that took you to the front door. Everything was white, outside of the contrasting window treatments.

Long rows of neatly trimmed bushes with soft colored lights gave the feeling of this being the kind of home one would find in a design studio for the elite. The cost for this home would be $5 million at least if it were anywhere in Los Angeles. Maybe ten, considering he hadn't been inside yet.

The front door opened, and a beautiful Indian woman in her thirties smiled at them with open arms. "Max, this is my wife, Vanya. Her name means gracious or god's gift. So, you can see, maybe we both have been blessed beyond what we might ever have imagined."

"So wonderful to meet you, Vanya. Thank you for welcoming me into your home."

"It is we who are thankful. Please make yourself at home." With this short greeting at the front door over, Vikram ushered them all inside.

The inside of Vikram's home was beyond spectacular. There were white pillars setting one room apart from the next, and gorgeous marble tiles throughout the house. Max's eyes were drawn to the art hanging on the walls. Incredible lifelike paintings of sacred deities and even a four-painting collection from the classic Kama Sutra. He didn't want to stare, but the photos were explicit and hard to turn away from. Beneath each photo was the Hindu Sanskrit meaning. The four photos depicted erotic love, desire, pleasure and beauty — the four tenants of the Kama Sutra.

Max's eyes were still roaming the walls and hallways of Vikram's home as he said, "Thank you so much. This is such an unexpected surprise." He looked down at his flea market wardrobe and couldn't help but notice Vikram and Vanya were dressed in stylish clothes even while being comfortable at home. "I feel very under dressed in my shorts and t-shirt. I was only prepared for a short trip to the bazaar."

Vanya smiled warmly at him. "Please, don't think of such a thing. We see travelers from all over the world. You will see, we are as casual as any American family."

Vanya called out to her daughters. "Savitri, Rhada, come welcome our guest. Please, first, go into the closet in your father's sports room and bring out something nice for him to wear. Something comfortable for dinner and overnight."

Max smiled at Vikram and Vanya. "Thank you again. You are mind readers."

In just a moment the two young women were standing with their mother, holding a True Religion sweatshirt and matching sweatpants. "Will this work?" Rhada asked as she handed the clothes to Max.

"Good choice, daughters." Vikram was so proud of his girls. "Max, these are my lovely girls, Rhada and Savitri."

"So wonderful to meet you. Hi, Rhada. Hi, Savitri. I'm Max. Thank you so much. You have good taste. True Religion is very popular in California."

"You're from Los Angeles? Do you know any famous movie stars?" Rhada held back while Savitri was brave enough to start asking their American guest questions.

"Girls, please. Our guest hasn't even made it to the family room yet. Why don't you offer him a glass of water or juice before you start asking him about movie stars?" Vanya wasn't stern, but managed to get her point across.

"Sorry, Mom. Sorry, Max. Can I get you a juice? We have apple, orange or cranberry," Rhada asked.

"Thank you, Rhada. Cranberry would be perfect."

Vikram, Vanya and Max walked to the sitting room just off the kitchen. In a minute, the girls were back with a tray of drinks and big smiles. They didn't seem sheltered by any means, but meeting an American from California was a treat for them.

It was easy to see how much Vanya and Vikram doted on their girls. "Thank you, Rhada," Vanya said. "Your father met Max on the train and he will be our guest for dinner and will be spending the night. Make sure he has whatever he needs."

The girls looked at each other, then answered in unison. "Yes, Mother." The girls were so beautiful and polite. They were raised with love and culture and their poise was well beyond their years. Max guessed they were maybe fourteen or fifteen.

"Welcome to our home, Max. After dinner can we ask you about life in California?" Savitri was as persistent as she was curious.

"I would love to tell you about California. I actually worked on a few TV shows and movies too. If it's okay with your parents, I would be happy to tell you some funny stories."

Max felt himself blushing at the kindness and sweet nature of these two beautiful young women. They were dressed in fun, happy clothes, t-shirts and jeans with designer sneakers. They had naturally beautiful long, dark hair that fell down over their shoulders. "If you all don't mind, can I change now? I love sweatshirts and these are great."

"Come with me," Savitri offered. "I'll show you." Savitri was excited to have an American guest. She took him by the hand and led him down the long hallway to one of three guest rooms.

She stopped at a hand carved door at the end of the hallway. "This is our best guest room. There is a waterfall shower, a big screen

TV, and a view of the garden. Fresh towels are on the bed and my mom said to tell you we will eat in thirty minutes."

"This is so amazing. Thank you, Savitri. I'll be ready."

Lunch was fit for a king. The dining room was expansive and members of the family's staff were busy placing new dishes on the table as they came out of the oven. Max sat at one end with Vikram and Vanya at the other. Savitri and Rhada sat next to Max on opposite sides of the table.

Dishes were passed around as crystal drinking glasses were filled with water and freshly made juices. Max reached for the large glass filled with a bright yellow juice. "What's this one, he asked?"

"Mango lassi," Rhada answered. "It's made of mangoes, yogurt, milk, ground cardamom and a pinch of sweetener. It's my favorite."

Max drank half of it down on his first sip. "Wow. This is so good. This is my best taste of India so far."

"And it's very healthy, Max. It's full of high-level probiotics." Vikram was happy to see his friend enjoy a real taste of India.

As they ate, the girls peppered Max with questions about Bali and Los Angeles, and he asked them about their life in India, high school and which movies they liked, of course.

Savitri was the more curious daughter. "Why did you come to India, Max? Are you here alone?"

"Savitri, that is a personal question." Vanya admonished, though she was not angry. She knew her daughters were curious, but a gentle reminder about being polite is the duty of a mother.

"I'm sorry Mom, Max."

Max didn't mind. He would have been happy to talk them all night. They were charming, intelligent, and fun to be around. "It's okay, really. I did come alone. My love life is a mess. But, I am hoping to go back to Bali with my girlfriend. If she's still my girlfriend."

"Did you breakup?"

This time, Vikram stepped in. "Rhada, you too? This after we just reminded your sister about personal questions?"

"Dad, Max said it's okay. Is it okay, Max?"

"Ha. Yes. It's okay. Love is tricky for all of us, regardless of age, right?

Savitri chimed in quickly. "It can be, but our parents try to make sure that doesn't happen."

"How do they do that?" Max asked.

Rhada, feeling the floor was open, supported her sister. "They arrange our marriages. We're doomed. From a very early age, we are told who we are going to marry and that's that."

Vanya threw a look at her lovely daughters as if to say, *Okay, that's enough.* It was a look they were familiar with.

"You know, the way my relationships have gone, I might have done a lot better if that happened in my life," Max said.

"And you think she is in India?" Rhada asked. "That's very exciting and romantic that you are looking for her."

"I know she's here. She's in Rishikesh at a yoga ashram. We're both trying to figure things out in our own way. Honestly, I don't know. I'm hoping to find all the answers. Being in the most spiritual place on earth can't hurt, can it?"

"All right, girls." Vanya looked at the empty plates and glasses, then motioned towards her daughters for some help to clear the table. "Max, your father and I will now have some alone time. You have things to do, yes?"

That was the clue to get up from the table. The girls made quick work of the dishes, then retreated to their rooms for some gossip and music. Max, Vikram and Vanya went out to the garden for tea.

CHAPTER SIXTEEN

Girls Just Want To Have Fun

Max's home in Bali was teeming with activity. He got a text from Fleur and Ali saying they had already landed and were enjoying the peaceful beauty of life at his villa. In between dips in the pool and wine in the jacuzzi, Fleur also managed to spend a day at Om Ham. She never did get to meet Master Ketut during the Dori and Max days, but when he noticed her sitting by herself in the gazebo area off the pool, he walked over to say hi.

"You're Max's young friend from a few years ago. What's your name?"

"Hi, Guru. Yes, it's me, Fleur. We never met officially, but you did give us a little advice after yoga class. It was when Dori and I were trying to figure out how to deal with Max after our little mix up."

"Ahhh....yes. I remember the *mix up* as you call it. Max is a bit of a troublemaker, isn't he?" Master Ketut said with a big smile. His inner love of Max as a friend and student was evident. "As I recall, you were all standing in the back of the yoga room, not knowing what to say to each other. Do you know why that is?" The Guru always asked questions that would help the person he asked to answer it themselves. He was just the intermediary.

"I think so," Fleur answered. "We all really liked each other and there was nothing to be mad about. Max and I had sex, but he was supposed to be here with Dori. He had no idea she was here, or even if she was coming here to meet him. We met up at this hostel, and we felt a real affection to one another. No one did anything with the intention of hurting anyone else. At least not on purpose. But… feelings did get hurt."

"You are a wise young woman, Fleur. Sometimes hurt feelings are inevitable. Maybe you will be a good partner for Max once again. He needs a good woman in his life." Master Ketut wore his usual grin as he spoke. He loved to push people to learn what they need to learn, to give advice or counsel when needed or asked for. Sometimes even when it's *not* asked, he would give it if he felts strongly enough about the person he was talking to. Even gurus don't love everybody equally.

"I don't know about that. I'm here with Ali, and we're both new to this girl thing, if that makes any sense. We've been partners for over a year and decided to live together in Los Angeles. Max has told me so many stories about you and the things you know about people just from meeting them, do you think we will be okay?"

"Love is good. Truth is good. Honesty with yourself is best. It's all good when it comes from the heart. I can't tell you who to love, or Max, or anyone. All I ever say is that when you fully trust your heart, the right answers are always there for you."

The Guru reached his hand towards Fluer's heart. "May I?"

"Yes, of course."

Master Ketut placed his right hand over Fleur's heart chakra. She could feel the heat from his hands.

"Is everything okay?" she asked nervously.

Master Ketut smiled and removed his hand from her heart and held it in hers. "You have a beautiful, healthy heart. It is pure, like your friend Max's. I told him that the first day I met him. It's a blessing in life, so listen to it."

"Thank you so much, Master Ketut. I'm so happy to be here and finally get a chance to talk to you."

The Guru just smiled. "I told Indra to give you a special massage. Afterwards, you will sit and have a coconut with me in the dining room. Okay?"

"Perfect. Thank you so much. It's reassuring to hear good news."

"Remember what I said. Be honest with yourself. You are not done with Max." With that, the Guru walked away to work in his garden.

Meanwhile at the villa

Ingrid walked through the French Doors in Max's bedroom that opened to the garden, pool and spa. She was in a flowery Bali wrap that covered her bikini bottoms. Somehow, she'd forgotten the top. Ali sat on the edge of the pool where it connected to the spa, her feet in the cool water up to her knees. It was a typical warm, sunny Bali afternoon — perfect for not much clothing and a pool to keep cool in.

"Hi, Ali. Thanks for inviting me over. It's a beautiful pool day, isn't it?"

Ali swung around to see her guest. She too was without a top. "'Girls just wanna have fun,' as the song goes. I decided to take your advice on being naked here."

"Why not?" Ingrid replied. "It's just us and the butterflies. And if you don't mind me saying so, you look beautiful."

"I don't mind at all," Ali said with a smile. Ali *was* a beautiful woman. Her long legs were tan and muscled and the suntan oil glistened on her breasts. The fresh air, the slight breeze combined to put her in natural state of arousal.

Ingrid didn't mean to stare, but her eyes lingered a little longer than she intended. "Mind if I sit?" she asked. Not waiting for a reply, she moved to the edge of the pool, peeled off her wrap and sat down next to Ali.

Two beautiful topless women at the pool. It could have been the South of France for all anyone would know. At least until the monkeys came in to steal a banana or two.

"I'm glad you could make it on such short notice. I hope you don't mind that Fleur isn't here."

"Where is she? I was thinking we could do some yoga together."

"Fleur went to Om Ham to get a massage, and I figured I would see if you were free today. Would you like a glass of wine?"

"That sounds great. Chilled white wine would be perfect."

Ali got up to get the drinks. "My kind of girl," she said as she walked into the house for refreshments.

Ali returned to the pool in short order with a bamboo tray covered in banana leaf. She brought out two glasses of wine, a small cheese board and a bowl of red and green grapes.

Ingrid reached for a glass and Ali raised hers for a toast. "To new friends and happy times." The girls clinked glasses and sipped.

"And happy endings," Ingrid added.

"You know..." Ingrid said with a wicked smile.

"What?" Ali asked interrupting her.

"I was thinking it's not really fair that Fleur is off getting a massage and here we are just sitting around at the pool."

"Well, she knew Max before any of us and she's been talking nonstop lately about seeing Master Ketut and being at Om Ham. So, it only makes sense for her to follow up on her opportunity."

"True enough. But such a long flight was probably just as stressful for you, right? We all deserve a good massage."

"I'm all for that, sister." The girls clinked glasses again and sipped. And sipped.

The more the girls drank, the more personal Ingrid's questions became. "So... how is it dating a younger woman?"

Ali wasn't sure where these questions were going, but she was turned on by Ingrid and wanted to explore while they were sitting there drunk and half naked. "Fleur's a really good girl. She's young and we were on a whirlwind of sorts when she first moved to L.A. One thing led to another. and when she asked if she could move in, I said yes. We got closer than I think either of us ever expected. I just don't know. I do love her, Ingrid, but sometimes I wonder if it's a passing romance or something that's meant to be."

"Do you regret it now?" Ingrid was trying to be a good friend. Or maybe trying to wiggle herself into Ali's life.

"Ahhh. I can't say that. It was a heartfelt choice at the time. Hey… Can we just enjoy the wine and the company?" Ali's response was honest, but she realized she may have already said too much.

"I'm sorry, Ali. That was a horrible question. Why don't we finish our wine, cool off in the pool, and then I will give you a soothing, relaxing massage that will clear your mind."

Ali didn't answer. Instead, she finished off her wine and jumped in the pool. When she came up for air, she looked at Ingrid. Her sultry smile returned. "What are you waiting for?"

Ingrid didn't have to say anything. She jumped into the pool. She swam up to Ali and put her hands on Ali's shoulders. They looked at each other for a moment, then kissed.

A short time later, the nearly full moon shed some light into the master bedroom Ali and Ingrid were in. Ingrid lit some incense and placed a couple of scented candles around the room. Thanks to the many trees in the backyard and the curtains, the bedroom had a romantic and sensual glow. It looked like a magical forest one would see in a dream.

"Oh, my god, that feels so good." Ali's face settled into a soft goose down pillow while Ingrid's long hands and nimble fingers worked slow, steady strokes up and down Ali's body. She poured drops of frangipani and lavender massage oil onto Ali's backside from her calves to her neck. Then, she let her hands roam all over, stopping only when she found a knot that needed some attention. Her hands moved slowly, sensually and with purpose. Ali was loose and pliable, and with each groan of pleasure she emitted, she encouraged Ingrid to explore more feely.

Ingrid lowered her bare chest onto Ali's back. She rubbed her breasts into the oil on Ali's back and glided up and down her body. Ali's legs parted just enough for Ingrid's fingers to find their way between her legs. She massaged Ali's butt, moving over the muscled mounds on each side, letting her fingers slide deeper between the crevices with each stroke.

Ali's moans became louder as Ingrid slid down Ali's body. They were body to body, then she turned Ali over onto her back. She worked her way up until her breasts were on top of Ali's. She fluttered the fingers of one hand between the strands of hair hanging over Ali's head, as one hand lingered between her thighs. They looked into each other's eyes, then kissed. They got lost in their kisses, tongues exploring tongues.

Ingrid moved her mouth lower, kissing Ali's neck then stopping on her breasts, licking, nibbling, using her most delicate touch. Ali's body was moving involuntarily beneath her. Her hips moved up and down with each movement of Ingrid's fingers. They were so lost in their seduction, neither one of them heard the front door open.

Fleur came back to the villa excited to tell Ali about her time with Master Ketut. What she came back to was not what she expected to find — Ali and Ingrid naked in the throes of passionate sex.

She watched them for a moment, silently, then dropped her purse to the wood floor. She purposely missed the faux fur area rug next to the bed. The soft thud startled Ali out of her primal state and into reality. Her head turned toward the sound. "Fleur." That was all she could get out.

Ingrid squirmed, then sat up next to Ali with her hands behind her. She pulled the covers up over their naked bodies. "Fleur," Ali said again.

"You said that already," Fleur threw back harshly. "I'm going back to Om Ham. Please finish what you started. I know from experience you tend to stop early." With that, Fleur walked out of the bedroom and through the still-open front door.

Ingrid and Ali heard her scooter drive away.

Fleur checked-in at the reception desk and was given the key to room 208. She could only shake her head. "Why is everything so weird here?" She asked herself out loud as she wondered what kind of universe gave her the very same room she got on her first night at Om Ham, when she'd met Dori right after making love to Max. *Maybe Master Ketut can help me with this one. Is this what they call Karma? Ha!*

She was tired, but in a good way. She was not going to let a most wonderful massage and talk with the guru go to waste by getting stressed out over Ali's indiscretion. Even though she was the younger of the two of them, she understood the sexual aspects of life in a pretty open-minded way. Maybe it was because she was French. Ali was an all-American woman, with all the American hang-ups to go with it. Women and men in France and Europe in general have lovers, and no one really gets upset about it. It's not like it's expected, but it's also not unexpected or frowned upon if it's done with class. Sex is sex. Love is a different state of mind.

She got undressed, got into her slightly oversized pajamas, and got comfortable in her bed. She pulled her phone from her purse, clicked on Max's name, then just stared at it. She wasn't sure what to say. She didn't want to talk to Ali. That was all she was sure of at the moment. She was surprised at her own ambivalence. She also hoped that's all there was to it and life would go on, as they say. One thing she knew for sure was she wasn't going to let anything get in the way of the beautiful day she just experienced.

CHAPTER SEVENTEEN

A New Day in New Delhi

Max stood under the rainforest shower that Savitri told him about when she brought him to his room. The water poured over him hot and steady. He adjusted the spray from massage to shower, back and forth, like a kid playing in the bath with his rubber ducks. He did slow neck rotations, stretched, and didn't want to get out. It was like being in a jungle without the wild animals.

There were tall plants in gorgeous ceramic pots in the corners of the massive marble shower enclosure. On various shelves, he found all kinds of loofah sponges, luxurious soaps and shampoos to indulge himself with. If he couldn't find Lea, maybe he come back and stay with Vikram and his family for a while.

He slept as well in his new surroundings as he had anywhere, even his own villa. He was happy to be at the breakfast table with Vikram, Vanya and the girls. She and her daughters made an American breakfast to give him a taste of back home. He was surprised and thrilled. He loved the food in Bali and other places in Indonesia, and he was adventurous so far in India, but sometimes a taste of home is just what the doctor ordered. Or Holy Man's wife, in this case.

A huge sterling silver bowl decorated with intricate drawings of elephants was the centerpiece of the table. There was a matching silver serving spoon and fork, with baby elephants for handles, stuck deep down into the dish that was filled with scrumptious looking scrambled eggs. The eggs looked light and fluffy, as if they'd been prepared for a chef's cooking show. Steam rose from the bottom of the bowl and the aroma of freshly cooked and chopped bacon bits were the only invitation Max needed.

He didn't eat meat as a personal choice, rather than because of a dietary issue, but he liked to abide by a quote from the late and profoundly loved guru, Baba Ram Das: "*It doesn't matter as much what goes into your mouth as what comes out of it.*"

There were side dishes of crispy hash browns, sliced onions, capers, and sourdough toast with heaps of butter and assorted jams. All homemade by Vanya's mother who brought them a nice assortment every time she visited from her home in Nepal. Best of all, there was a carafe of hot dark roast coffee. Vikram was not only a holy man, but a psychic as well.

"I have to ask you, Vanya. How did you know about crispy hash browns?"

"It wasn't me. The girls, Rhada in particular, spent the night way past their bedtimes looking up popular breakfast items and trendy breakfast eateries in Los Angeles. They even called this one called NATS, to ask how certain items were prepared. It's a Jewish Delicatessen near your old home, right?" As Vanya spoke, she gave the girls the eye when she got to the part of their staying up way too late. In Max's eyes, it was funny and sweet to see.

"Ha. That's amazing. Yes. I'm Jewish and it's a very popular and hip breakfast joint. I can't tell you how it all started, but for some reason, it seems many Jewish people have this thing about ordering their hash browns burnt on each side."

Max looked directly at the girls. "Rhada, Savitri, thank you so much. I used to teach high school part time, and I would have never quit if I had students like you. I'm so happy to have met you both."

"Same here, Max." Savitri was smiling as she talked. "It was fun for us to meet you and hear some of your stories. We also wish you good luck with finding your girlfriend. Please bring her here if you do, okay?"

"I would love to. I have to find her first, of course, but I know she would love to meet you."

Vikram looked at his girls. "Savitri, could you and your sister please take your plates to the patio. Your mother and I want to talk with Max a little more before he leaves on his journey."

The girls got up and each one gave Max a very sweet hug and a kiss on the cheek to say good-bye. They took their plates to the patio deck out back, leaving Max and their parents to talk.

"You look well rested and ready for a new day. Have you decided on anything?" Vikram had offered him a ride to the bazaar or his hotel, whatever he wanted.

"I'm not sure, Vikram. I was going to take the train to the airport and fly to Rishikesh to begin my search for Lea. But now I'm not so sure that's what I want to do."

"Why is that? Did something change your mind?" Vanya wanted to know in case there was a way she or her husband could help. "I don't mean to pry."

"It's totally okay. You're not prying. I slept great, but I did have a couple of short, unusual dreams. One of them was about an old girlfriend from about five years ago. When she stopped seeing me, it really broke my heart. I didn't go out on a date for almost four years after that."

"That's a long time. When you were together, did you talk about marriage or family?" Vanya was direct in her questions and open to talk about intimate subjects. It helped Max feel free to be honest and speak from his heart.

"Marriage, yes. We never talked about family. I was kind of relieved in that sense. She was and still is a free spirit. Having a dog was good enough for both of us."

"It's good to know yourself in that way. Not everyone is meant to have children."

"I felt the same. It wasn't an issue for me. Sometimes I felt that if I met a woman who had a child who was already past the toddler years, that would be good. Anyway, we weren't a match in a lot of ways. It just took time for me to see things clearly."

Vanya got the sense that Max had reached his limit for talking about his relationships. "You know what they say… it's never too late for anything we want in our lives."

"I get it. Honestly, it's difficult for me to know the real answer, if that makes any sense. She told me she loved me on our third date. I was a little hesitant, because we had a 22-year age difference. But I said it back. And I was happy I did."

"Age means nothing," Vikram said. "Here in India, a 20 year difference is nothing. Sometimes, it's much more and sometimes in arranged marriages the couple can be very close or very far apart in age. True love does not come with an age requirement, but circumstances can make for unusual partnerships."

"I didn't care about that. We could sit and talk for hours. Right after our first date, she began to text me every morning just to say 'hi, I just got up. I'm going to the gym or the market.' It made me laugh. I never had that before in all my years of dating. For me, it felt so good to be needed.

"When she told me she was in love with someone else, someone even older than me, I understood that being needed is not the same as being loved. I still think about her every once in a while, but not in a way that upsets me or gets in my head about my happiness or current relationships. A thought will come and go in a matter of seconds. She's not a part of my life in anymore. I fooled myself more than I ever thought possible. Love can do that to a person, right?"

Vanya was as wise as she was beautiful. "The wisest of sages have been fooled in matters of love. And who is to say you were fooled, Max.?"

Vikram added, "You are not alone, brother. Love grabs our heart and it's a feeling that can make us so happy we lose sight of other things."

Vanya had a smile and story for Max. "Mata Hari fooled Kings and Queens and the greatest of generals on the battlefield. She gave them the illusion of love in exchange for secrets that helped her side win many battles. What is important now is how you go forward."

"I know. I'm sorry. I'm not complaining. I've been so blessed. I was so loved by my late wife, Dori, I could never again let myself be with a woman who didn't love me as I loved her."

Vikram moved from his seat across from Max, to sit next to him on the sofa. He reached his hands out over Max's lower chakras. "May I move my hands over you and gently touch your heart and sacral chakras?"

"Sure. I've done Reiki sessions before and my body is very responsive."

"Wonderful. Please lie back and close your eyes. Take long deep breaths."

Max did as he was told, and Vikram moved his hands in circular and up and down motions over Max's body. He stopped for a few seconds in some spots, whispered prayers of sorts, then left his hands over Max's navel for a long moment.

"You may sit up now. Thank you for trusting me."

"Anything out of the ordinary?" Max asked.

"You have some blockages in your sacral and heart chakras. If you want to postpone your trip to Rishikesh for one day, I would like you to stay here. I will have Devi drive you to see a very special friend of mine who is a trusted healer and medicine woman in a small village not too far from here. Devi will take you and wait for you to bring you back. Then you will rest for the night. I think it will help you a great deal in your search for answers. And the girls will be so happy to badger you with more questions. What do you say?"

"Yes. I would like that very much. When will this happen? I still need to go to my hotel, check out, get my passport and things."

"No problem. I will call my friend Lady Aahana, and Devi will get you where you need to go and back here for dinner with us. Vanya wants to prepare a special Indian meal for your last night."

"Wear the outfit from last night and if you have any yoga pants or loose comfortable clothing in your backpack, that is all you will need. If not, we will stop and get you something on the way. Take a few minutes in your room to freshen up and Devi will be in the driveway in an hour."

Max felt like he was walking on a cloud. "Thank you so much. I'll go change and be ready for Devi. Is there anything else I need to know? Anything to be nervous about?"

"Just breathe, relax, enjoy the ride to the country. You will be in kind and loving hands. If you have a question of her, ask it. She will answer."

Max let out one of his famous long sighs. "All-righty."

Morning at Om Ham

Fleur was up with the roosters. She slept pretty well, considering she went to bed with the vision of her naked girlfriend making love to a mutual guest of theirs at the villa. She reached for her phone and immediately noticed it was still on the WhatsApp page with a message written to Max that was not sent. *Hmm. Accident or divine intervention?* she wondered. *Coffee first,* she decided. Just like her old friend from the mountains.

She put on a soft, white, oversized t-shirt. She loved room to move. This shirt came down to her mid thighs, and would cover her if she didn't want to wear anything else. What could be better?

Just as she walked out the door, her phone chimed with a text message. It was Ali. Fleur sat down at the very same bistro table where she'd sat when she first met Dori just after making love with Max in the room below theirs. This was before any of them knew the craziness that they would all inadvertently be part of. She laughed out loud. "Oh Dori. You were sweet and an angel. Max and I were both lucky to know you. Here I am now, in my old room next to yours, and let me tell you, you would not believe what just happened."

Her phone chimed again, loud enough to snap her out of her fog. She realized she was talking out loud to herself, not that anyone would care anyway. The guests at Om Ham were all high in one way or another with yoga or swimming, doing their own thing, and not paying too much attention to others. That's one of the reasons she liked being there. The text from Ali said, "Can we talk?"

Fleur's phone rang. It was Ali. Apparently, she was not going to let an unanswered text stop her. "Yes?" Fleur was short and her voice was not as sweet sounding as it was known to be.

"Can I come over to Om Ham and meet you for breakfast? We should talk and not let any crazy thoughts get exaggerated. Thirty minutes?"

"Sure. Come to the Tulsi. I'll be upstairs at the corner table."

Ali felt relieved even if she was unsure of how Fleur was going to handle what happened. "Great. Thank you. See you in thirty."

CHAPTER EIGHTEEN

Max, Fleur, Ali
and a Healer in New Delhi

The shiny new and slightly out of place Mercedes Maybach rounded curve after curve leaving the city behind for an almost jungle like flora that could easily have a person wondering where civilization was. In some ways, it reminded him of being lost in one of the many rice terraces of Bali or darting in and out of a jungle like area that was only a few meters from the main road.

"Are we getting close to where the healer lives?" Max was curious. He hoped he didn't sound nervous, or worse, like a child asking "are we there yet?" He had seen a couple of healers in Bali, but he knew of them beforehand, and knew friends who had gone before him. This was different. He was again, a stranger in a strange land. He was on a quest, looking for love in the land of Dharma, Karma, and chicken masala.

There were tall trees, thick bushes, and probably an interesting assortment of wildlife crawling through it all. Every few minutes they passed a cluster of village style thatched roof huts and shanty style structures where young children played in front of their homes with their mothers nearby pounding flour, milking goats, tending to whatever was growing in their gardens. It was lightyears from the luxury estate he just left an hour ago.

"You seem nervous. Let me assure you there is nothing to worry about." Devi was doing his best to reassure Max that he was meeting someone special and that Vikram has only his best interests at heart.

"Thank you, Devi. I'm not really nervous. I'm just not quite sure why I am even doing this. I feel good though."

"Ha… everyone says they feel good on the way to the doctor's office. Relax. I will be here waiting for you when you come out."

"Easy for you to say, you'll be sitting in a fabulous limousine listening to music and smoking your pipe."

The car stopped in front of beautiful wood frame house surrounded by flowers. The road was paved and there was a Buddha sculpture in the middle of a vegetable garden opposite a fountain adorned with small angel sculptures with wings. The peaceful energy was welcome.

Devi opened the door. Max stepped out and reached into his pocket. Devi stopped him. "Everything is taken care of. The master is a gracious host and this is his treat for his new American friend. Please go in with all our blessings. Do whatever Lady Aahana tells you. She is our secret treasure."

Back at Om Ham with Fleur and Ali

Fleur played with her bamboo straw as she sipped a dragon fruit smoothie. She wasn't really hungry and could only manage to use her fork to push around the stir fry tofu on her plate. Her cigarette days were over. Food was now her stress reducer. She took in a deep breath and let it out, a-la her dear friend Max. "Max, where are you?" She said to no one. "I need you." In the good old days of a couple of years ago, they would have shared a doobie. That sweet thought made her smile. *Maybe we will again. Master Ketut said we weren't done.*

Ali walked up to her table. The timing was perfect. Fleur had a smile on her face. "Hey, sweetie. You look happy." Ali was hoping Fleur had already forgotten about yesterday, or at least turned the page.

Fleur turned around to see Ali standing at the empty chair next to her. "You can sit. I'm happy enough."

Ahhh. So much for that thought, Ali realized.

Ali sat down next to Fleur. They were friends who'd hung out and laughed together for almost two years after they met at Max and Dori's wedding. They got close living together when Fluer took a long vacation to Los Angeles and stayed with her. Soon, the relationship changed from friends to lovers, and then from lovers to partners who had thoughts of working together on new business projects.

"I'll go first," Ali said. "I'm truly sorry, Fleur. I'm not going to say something stupid like, 'it just happened, or it didn't mean anything.'"

"Okay," Fleur replied.

She's obviously going to make me work for this. Ali thought. "I was horny, Ingrid is gorgeous and sexy, and I wanted to have sex. Can we work from that point of view?"

"Yes, we can. It's honest. It's true." Fleur let out a little laugh. "I would fuck her too if she came onto me."

Ali laughed with her friend, feeling like they'd crossed over some of their tension. "She does have that effect on people," Ali said.

"I don't know how Max resisted all these years." Ali was trying to move past it quickly. Fleur was not necessarily buying it.

"You know, I saw you give your phone to Ingrid to exchange contacts. It was sneaky. You did it when I went to the bathroom and you were alone with her. That bothered me. It bothered me a lot more than the sex I figured you would get around to. Who knows? If we had that group yoga session Ingrid mentioned, we all might have enjoyed a fun, sensual threesome."

Ali's eyes brightened along with her smile. "That would be beautiful. It would be something new for us. You're right about the phone number thing. I feel bad."

"Last night I had a great talk with Master Ketut after my massage. He said some very interesting things to me."

Now it was Ali who was curious and a little insecure about what might come next. If she had any doubts about her relationship with Fleur, there was a good chance Master Ketut felt them and shared his thoughts during their talk. "Tell me," she said.

"First off, he told me that I was healthy and had a pure heart. He said I will be my happiest self when I'm able to look at the past as my best opportunity to learn more about myself. Then we got into my life going forward. He said I would be back in Paris and that I was not done with Max."

"Not done? What does that mean?" Ali was more than curious.

Fleur took a sip of her smoothie. "I don't know yet. I did think about him last night, and I started a text message to him that I ended up not sending. It's still on my phone."

"Okay. That's pretty big. Do you think you want to be with him again?"

"I don't know, Ali. The times we did have sex it was just two strangers meeting in a remote romantic spot on a mountain. I was lonely and needed company. My father had just died and I ran to Bali. I didn't know what I was doing. Max was there and he was the best friend the universe could have sent me at that time."

"Shit. I heard the story from Dori many times, but never from your perspective. That feels like a lifetime ago to me, but it sure seems front and center to you. Do you still have feelings for him?"

"Ali, please. That's too much for me to think about right now. It was almost two years ago. Look, I'm not mad at you."

"But…" Ali said.

Fleur continued, "But, sometimes just one little thing can cause such a huge chain reaction of thoughts. It made me wonder if I really want to live in Los Angeles."

"Really? I thought you loved living in Los Angeles."

"It's okay. I prefer Paris, actually. And, it's not so much about being with you, because that's been amazing…most of the time." She looked at Ali after she said that. "I'm sorry. I didn't mean that to be mean. I hate when people hold things over me like I did something so wrong and unforgivable that I should be thankful they still talk to me. Fuck that. Now, I just did it to you."

"It's all right, Fleur. You don't have a mean bone in your body. I agree with you how sometimes one event, one word, can make any of us rethink our lives."

Fleur felt relieved that Ali was being so understanding. "Thank you, Ali, for saying that. Master Ketut just laid it all out for me. His words made me think about all of my relationships, especially my family."

That comment landed with a thud. Ali was speechless. She sat back in her chair hoping the right words or thoughts would come to her. Now.

Fleur pushed away from the table. "I'm going to spend the day here, swim, drink from coconuts, relax."

"All right. That sounds like a good idea. Have fun, enjoy the pool. I'm going to finish my tea and head into town to Bali Buddha. I was thinking of cooking tonight. I can make that grilled tempeh steak you love so much, and get some ice cream for desert. Would you like that?"

Fleur couldn't stop the half smile that creased her face like clockwork at the mention of ice cream. But still, she was not ready. "I'll text you later if I can make it.

Ali's hopefulness faded. "All right. I hope I see you later. Take whatever time you need."

Back in New Delhi Inside with Lady Aahana

Lady Aahana opened the door to her home. She stepped out onto the top step, a beautiful stone tablet like step with doves painted in the corners and the words God and his Angels reside here and everywhere. The words were embedded into the stone in all the colors of the rainbow. Next to the top step there was a wooden shelf to place your shoes.

Lady Aahana looked like one of the angels he just passed at the fountain. Her head was shaved. Glittering earrings dropped from each ear. An amulet made with large black onyx and rose quartz hung at the center of her chest. There was an aura of power that surrounded her.

Her eyes were like a magnet, daring you to look away. It was either turn back now, or full steam ahead as the conductor would shout. Max was ready. He had been in temples like this before, standing with people who also held energetic powers in their hands. It was a little unnerving, but he knew Vikram would not send him somewhere to someone who was not safe.

She wore a white robe with dazzling crystals around her wrists. Max could make out the Amethyst, the amber and the rose quartz. The rest he would have to ask about. "Welcome to my home, Max. Please come in."

Lady Aahana took his hands in hers. Max could feel her heat and the healing powers within her. She led him inside and closed the door behind them.

The room was calming. There was a hand-crafted massage table in the far corner of the room. It was covered in a luxurious white cotton cloth and surrounded by big crystals and deep green plants.

Next to the massage table, was a beautiful red leather sofa in the shape of a heart. Lady Aahana pointed to it. "Sit with me. I would like to talk to you before we start our session. Please don't hold back any thoughts or emotions. You're here for a reason. Let's find out what it is."

CHAPTER NINETEEN

Enjoying Om Ham

Face down on a pool lounge chair, Fleur's breathing slowed her mind and body. The tension was fading. She was not one to hold a grudge, and she was not uptight about sex. The part that played over and over in her mind was the way Ali slipped Ingrid her phone when she thought they were alone.

She didn't get it. She and Ali were good friends. They laughed a lot, ate a lot of ice cream sitting on the sofa while watching movies, and from what Fleur could tell, they kept very little from each other as their relationship grew. They talked about everything from sex with Max to politics in America. Sex with Max was the better topic by a long shot, even though Ali did not have any first-hand experience. Her stories were strictly hearsay. And for right now, this moment, she wanted them to stay that way.

Fleur's breathing may have slowed down, but her mind was still racing a mile a minute. It wasn't just thoughts about Ali and Ingrid, it was everything. She was only 32 but looked 20 — a baby herself in the eyes of others. She still missed her dad, who was her best friend until the day he died. She missed her mom and sisters and wondered if they felt she had abandoned them.

She was so lost in her thoughts, she didn't hear the voice coming from the person sitting on the chair next to hers. Finally, a hand touched her shoulder. "Excuse me," a soft American voice said.

Fleur looked up, and a few strands of long blonde hair fell into her line of sight.

"I'm sorry to bother you," the young man continued. "I left my wallet under the lounge chair. I didn't want to stick my hand under there without saying something."

Fleur was awake now. She sat up and looked up to the handsome face and blue eyes of a young man around her age, or maybe a little younger. She wasn't too tired to take note of his lean, tan body. "Hi. That's okay. Thank you for saying something. I might have screamed if I had seen an arm reaching up under my chair."

"My name is Brian," the young man said. His eyes were having a hard time looking only at Fleur's smile. As hard as he tried, it was still obvious. She could feel the intensity of his gaze and was fully aware her breasts were partially hanging out of her bathing suit.

"My name is Fleur." She sat up and tucked a little more of herself into her bathing suit, even though modesty was not her strong suit. "Would you like to sit or are young going to take your wallet and run?"

"You're funny. Are you from France?"

"Yes. Paris. Have you been?"

"No, not yet. I've been to Nice and St. Tropez, but that was just a few days at the beach." Brian sat down at the very edge of Fleur's lounger. "I hope I get the opportunity to spend more time really exploring France."

"I hope you do. It's the center of the universe. At least for me," Fleur added."

Brian got up, wallet in hand. "Well, have a great day. Sorry if I disturbed you."

Fleur reached for her bag as she sat up. "Are you doing anything now?"

"Nothing in particular. I was just here for a swim. Why?"

"I was thinking, instead of swimming, maybe we could do something together. Let me give you a hint. I already ate."

"I have a room here. Would you like to come up?" Brian said as he caught on.

Fleur was thankful for that. She wasn't offering any resistance to this sexy young surfer, but a woman does have a limit as to how far she will go in these sorts of things, *n'est pas?*

Fleur smiled up at him, holding her hand out for him to reach for. "Help a lady up, will you? I'll do the same for you later."

Brian looked seductively at her wearing a teenager's grin and thinking of what comes next. "I won't need any."

Soon thereafter, Brian stood in front of Fleur, naked as the day he was born, and as confidant as a porn star. She sat on the edge of the bed, unable to hold back a smile as she devoured him with her eyes. It had been a while since she was with a man. In this moment, she wondered why.

Her hands rested on his chest as she kissed his nipples. First one, then the other. He swayed, his knees bending, his excitement showing. She moved her hands lower to touch him. She looked up at him to connect with his alluring blue eyes, then her mouth moved lower. Slowly. She's French after all.

Brian pushed gently on Fleur's shoulders, easing her back flat onto the bed. He kissed her lips, then her neck. He moved lower to her breasts, kissing her passionately. Her legs opened for him and he fit himself inside her. They moved together, riding a wave of pleasure until they were just a configuration of limbs that finally fell to their sides as their last gasps of pleasure escaped their mouths.

CHAPTER TWENTY

Rishikesh

Max sat patiently in the waiting area for his 55-minute flight to Dehradun's Jolly Grant Airport in Rishikesh. It was only a short taxi ride to the ashram from there, and he would find out soon enough if Lea was still here working on her yoga practice or something else entirely.

His text messages were going unanswered, but that didn't bother him. He was *in India*. He would either find her or not. They would work things out, or not. Either way he would have an opportunity to do something he had only dreamt about until now — be in a real yoga ashram in India. *What the heck,* he thought, *if Julia Roberts could to it in* Eat, Pray, Love, *I can do it as I continue my journey of love. If it was good enough for the Beatles and Ram Das, it will be good enough for me.* He also had another thought. *If only Satya could see me now. My India is actually in India! Take that!*

Max was silent in his thoughts. Although his time in New Delhi was short, it had left a lasting impression that started to dawn on him.

The flight from Bali to New Delhi started his adventure only a week ago. Meeting a holy man on the train to the bazar he never got to see, was life changing. Vikram and his entire family and his personal driver all welcomed him with open arms and hearts. They shared stories over food and drinks and showed him a side of life in India that he would have otherwise never seen.

But most of all, the meeting with Vikram's friend, the healer Lady Aahana, was what had him waiting for his flight with both anticipation and a bit of nervous wonderment. He was asking himself questions he had not asked in a very long time. Questions that he realized there were no answers to even though human nature will cause us to ask once in a while.

The memory of his time with her was still fresh in him mind. Right after meeting her and talking about why he was there, she had him lie on her table. He was naked other than a soft towel to cover his privates and an assortment of healing crystals. A fist-sized Amethyst crystal bathed in deep violet and purple hues sat squarely on his chest in his heart space. Next to it, was a smaller sized Rose Quartz crystal, known for its healing powers in matters of emotional injury such as self-love and self-acceptance.

On his head, Lady Aahana placed a smaller Clear Quartz crystal, which is known as the *master healer* because it helps align all the chakras and energetically attune to other crystals. Tourmaline was placed on his belly to protect against negative energy as well as help with stress and anxiety.

He took in a long, deep, slow breath, held it for a count of three, then exhaled slowly until his lungs were empty. Then he laughed to acknowledge his weirdness. To the other people in the waiting area, he was just another American talking to himself.

Lady Aahana worked from the crown chakra over his head all the way down to his root chakra just below the base of the spine. When his session was over, she told him she went deeper than usual with new clients, but only where she was guided. She cleared out old patterns and negative energies while his body responded by twitching around on the table and at a few points, even moving an inch or two off the table completely.

She had seen this happen many times, and it gave her a good feeling inside that her work was being received. If a person is open and receptive to this kind of healing, the results can be life changing and profound. It can move people into the direction they have wanted to move to for a long time but were prevented by their own blocks and limitations.

When his session was over, he felt great. Lady Aahana told him he was clear and just as Master Ketut would say, to follow his heart. "There is no right or wrong, Max. Only choices we make that lead us to one place or another."

Her words stuck with him while he waited to hear his boarding call. She didn't give him any insight into finding Lea or what would happen if he did, but she did say one thing that he could not forget: "There is a deep pain within you, Max, that blocks you from the freedom to the love that you sometimes *think* you have. Until you let go of it and forgive whomever including yourself, no matter where it comes from, love will be a tricky illusion for you — a balancing act of walls between you and others that you keep up and let down. When they are down, your life is filled with sweet love. When they go back up, you drift and keep people at arm's length. Go in peace, Max. What you need will present itself. Quiet your mind and it will find you."

The bell sound of a WhatsApp message brought him back to the present. He pulled his phone from his back pocket and saw the text from Fleur:

> Max. Where are you? Everything is okay at the villa, but not between Ali and me. I walked in on her and Ingrid having sex. Can you imagine?

Max loved when Fleur said that, but not when it meant imagining something bad. *"Can you imagine?"* He could picture the expression on her face and hear her words in her deliciously beautiful French accent. His phone chimed again.

> Can I come to India and help you look for Lea? I could use the escape. I also miss you.

> Xoxoxo Fleur.

Ingrid. Max wasn't surprised. *She's hard to resist.* Ali surprised him though, especially after talking to her and Fleur and hearing how excited they were about starting a business together.

The time stamp of the messages was from much earlier in the morning. Middle of the night morning. He took a moment, then typed his response.

> Fleur. I would love to see you. It's a very long flight to New Delhi and I'm already on my way to Rishikesh. Please take some time, let things quiet down a bit, and see how you feel in another day or so. Maybe take a day or two at Om Ham. That always helps me.

> Let me know if I can help you with anything there.

> In the meantime, Je t'aime.

> Your friend, always, Max.

"Now boarding flight twelve twenty to Rishikesh." The announcement was listing the rows for boarding, starting with elite status and other categories that board first, just like everywhere else.

Max took a few steps toward the gate agent when his phone chimed again. He looked down at the new message.

> Love you, sweet Max. I am at Om Ham now. I feel better.

> Will you tell you more later.

> Ciao.

Max smiled as he read the message. He loved Fleur and would never forget the passion she brought back into his life when he needed it most. He was happy she was at Om Ham. He hoped she would find the same comfort there that he did.

Ha! If only he knew. Sometimes they are like twin flames who have not realized it yet.

CHAPTER TWENTY-ONE

Parmarth Niketan Ashram

The driver stopped at the walkway leading up to Parmarth Niketan. Max exited the beat-up old taxi, put a generous tip in the driver's hands, and whispered a heartfelt thank you. When the driver pulled away, he was covered, for a moment, in a blanket of exhaust fumes coming from the run-down engine. Once the smoke cleared, he was standing in front of the ashram with a clear view of the massive school.

The enormity and godliness of the structure overwhelmed him. Young and old alike, men and women, children, beggars, sadhus, more humanity than he could ever identify or imagine, all wandered in and out of the various buildings, restaurants, and small kiosks selling religious and spiritual items.

The Ganges river bank was close enough to see and hear. It's a sacred river to Hindus and now he was standing close enough to put his feet into it. That thought moved him forward. He sat on the edge not far from where children were playing in the water and life floated by. In the famous book, *Siddhartha,* written by Herman Hesse, it says: *"If you sit on the edge of the Ganges long enough, you will see your own soul float by."* That was a theory Max was not going to test. He had things to do.

Max entered the main building to begin his search for Lea, his adventure, or his whatever it would turn out to be. Yoga rooms were everywhere. All a person had to do was follow any number of arrows.

Arrows to Hatha Yoga and Vinyasa yoga were the most popular. Meditation rooms, prayer halls and vegetarian cafes were abundant. He took a deep breath, then followed the first arrow to Hatha Yoga for teachers. Lea was an advanced student and it was likely she would be in a teacher study group or something similar.

"Class in session", the sign read. There was an older Indian man, at least seventy if Max had to guess, who smiled kindly at him as he looked at the closed door.

"One hour, please. There are other classes starting just down the hall. Join any open door. Welcome to Parmarth Niketan."

"Thank you," Max replied. "Is there a restaurant you would recommend, and are there tours of the Ashram?"

The old man smiled. "Walk wherever your heart takes you. Ask questions. Anyone here will be happy to help you. Try the Green Room, it's a wonderful vegetarian restaurant with a buffet that offers the best of Indian food." With that, the old man wandered off down one of the hallways that led to countless open areas where people sat in group meditation, in silent prayer, or doing service. Service was an exchange for living at the ashram and taking classes, and could be cleaning floors, bathrooms, doing dishes, anything that the ashram needed to stay clean and be the sanctuary it was known for world wide.

Max followed the old man until he came to an opening that lead into a courtyard. In just a few steps, he saw people carrying trays of food and drinks. He walked up to a woman wearing a long, white peasant dress and sandals, with a beautiful lace shawl over her head. He tapped her on the shoulder. "Hi. Excuse me."

She turned around to face him and he had to laugh to himself. The first person he talked to at the ashram was wearing a sign that said, "I am in silence."

She smiled politely at him. He was immediately captured by her aura of calmness and by her beauty in the physical sense. She had sparking green eyes and gorgeous long brown hair hanging well below her shawl. Her smile was warm and friendly. She looked at peace with the world. She motioned for him speak.

"Hi. Thank you. I was wondering where the cafe is. I see people walking with trays of food and drink. I just arrived an hour ago."

She smiled and held up a finger to ask for a moment, then took a note pad from her pocket and wrote something. "Hi. Welcome." Then she took out a note that she had prepared for such occasions. "I'm Jenny, from San Diego." Then she pointed behind her to the next hallway and courtyard.

"Thank you. I'm Max. I'm from Los Angeles, but mostly I live in Bali. I hope I see you again when you're talking."

Jenny laughed. She bowed politely, then wrote "You're welcome" on her note pad. She showed it to him, smiled, and walked away.

Back at Om Ham

Fleur looked at the text message from Ali.

> Let's have dinner together. I'm making something special.
>
> Please come.
>
> I love you.

Fleur gathered herself together, looked around her room one final time and walked out.

She sat at reception to work out a meditation and yoga program for a week. She decided it would be good for her and it would give her and Ali some guaranteed space between them so they could each get into a routine that would give them happy, positive time to be alone with themselves. It had been too long since they did that.

She had moments wondering about this new business venture Ali wanted her to commit to. It would be a big responsibility that would require time and dedication together for it to be successful. She worried that they had not known each other long enough to make this kind of decision. Master Ketut told her to take a week for yoga, meditation and healing. And that's exactly what she was going to do.

Eluh put the weeklong Harmony and Healing package in front of Fleur. She outlined the seven-day program detailing when the massage treatments were and the consultation times with Master Ketut. She pointed out when she needed to be at the ashram across the street for cleansing ceremonies and silent time in the cave.

Fleur was excited and eager to begin this week of healing. She wasn't sure about the silent time in the cave. *That's not my thing,* she thought. *But, maybe…* Then, she smiled.

Fleur's phone rang. It was Ali. She picked up anyway. The anger from the moment had faded. The pleasurable afternoon with Brian had lightened her mood and her spirits. "Hi Ali. I'm at Om Ham."

"Ahh. Are you staying? I want you to come home. I miss you."

"I miss you too," Fleur replied quickly. She started to say something but Ali jumped back in without waiting for her to finish.

"Cool. What time will you be home?"

"Actually, I'm staying here for now. I decided to take a week-long meditation and healing program here with the Guru. I need it. I'm not mad at you. You hurt my feelings partying with Ingrid. But, also I know enough to understand that I could have just walked into the room when you and Ingrid were exchanging phone contacts and then who knows?"

"Wow. Fleur. A week? I wasn't expecting that. Maybe I should just go home."

"I don't know what to tell you. You have to do what feels right for you."

There was a moment of silence.

"Hey… I have to get settled into my new room. My first massage is in an hour. Tonight will be my first meditation. I think it's sound healing in the main yoga room. I'll talk to you later, Ali. I promise."

Ali was dejected but put her best self forward, being kind and gracious. "That sounds lovely, Fleur. I'm happy you're doing something for yourself." She wasn't sure if that's what she really thought though. Right from the beginning, she knew the age difference between them could present itself when it was least expected and for sure, least wanted.

Fleur's voice was also kind and hopeful. "I'll call you in a couple of days, Ali. I'm just going to hang out here. I want to talk to Max. He's in Rishikesh now, and he always knows what to say to help me feel better. So… be good to yourself as well. It's all good. I love you. See you soon."

She wasn't too sure if that's what she would do though. Ali knew much more about what she wanted in her life. She was accomplished and had her career, and on and on. Fleur was still growing, unsure of her path forward. And now, she had so many questions. She put her phone away. *Time to unwind.*

Ali had set the dining table before Fleur called. She was being positive, manifesting what she wanted, living it out as if it were inevitable. We never know when it will work out that way. The monogrammed carved wood placemats were out and the good wine glasses were in front of each plate. A beautiful candelabra in the shape of two women intertwined decorated the center of the table. It was all for naught, as they say. She grabbed one of the wine glasses and filled it from the open bottle that she started when she set the table.

Ali was older than Fleur by twelve years. It's not a lot of years in the linear sense, but a lot can happen in a short amount of time that shapes our life experiences on a much deeper level than any set number of years on a calendar. She knew Fleur was dealing with a lot when she first invited her to move in, but she also felt a connection with her that went beyond offering comfort. That proved to be an accurate assumption. In a short time together, a spark was ignited that changed their friendship into a passionate romance.

Ali took a long sip from her wine glass, noting she'd just about finished the bottle. She stared longingly at the unopened bottle, as if it were a friend that would come to her aid. She was in a long-term relationship with a younger woman, and trying to rid herself of the guilt she was feeling over her little tryst with Ingrid.

She opened the second bottle carefully, then filled her wine glass to the rim. She took a sip, then put it down. She felt the emptiness of the beautiful space they were supposed to be enjoying together. She walked toward the garden spa with her wine glass in one hand, disrobing with the other. When she got to the edge of the spa, her naked silhouette slid into the moonlit water.

CHAPTER TWENTY-TWO

The Ashram

Max ordered the channa masala and a side plate of chicken shawarma. He'd planned to use his savory garlic naan bread to wipe up whatever was left on his plate. It was almost embarrassing to note when he looked down that there was nothing left to wipe up. It was bone dry. It looked like had been passed around to a couple of hungry dogs to lick clean before being taken to the kitchen. The food had been that good.

"Kirtan at seven with Lea," the sign said. Max couldn't believe it, and no one would probably believe it if he told them. He was wandering the hallways looking for an administrative office to ask if his friend, a yoga teacher, might have signed up for a workshop. He was hoping for a clue or even a list of the class schedules. But this… Wow! He looked up and said, "Thank you guides, thank you angels, thank you GOD!

Max looked at his phone to check the time. It was still early — four in the afternoon. He had plenty of time to go to the registration desk and ask about a room on campus.

"Welcome to Parmarth Niketan. How may I help you?" The woman's voice was kind and friendly. Her name tag said Audrey. She looked to be in her fifties and reminded him of his fraternity house college days when there was always a kindly older mom who came around to cook their meals and be a mom away from home for those who needed her.

"I'm Max. So nice to meet you. I would like to get a room for three days. Maybe longer if it's possible."

"Wonderful. Nice to meet you. I hope you will enjoy your stay. Are you here to meet with a particular guru or teacher training program?"

"Not right now. I'm actually looking for a friend of mine from Bali. She got her teacher training credential here and I just noticed she is leading a Kirtan group tonight at seven."

"Your friend is Lea?"

"Yes. I would like to sign up for her class. I'm hoping we can talk afterwards and she can recommend a few classes for me during my stay here."

Audrey handed him a sign-up sheet to add his name. "That will be 850 rupees. We accept any Visa card if you did not get a chance to change money. It's about eleven US dollars."

Max handed her 900 rupees. He still had a pocket full, considering the huge difference in dollars to rupees. "Thank you, Audrey."

"Enjoy your Kirtan, Max. Lea is a favorite here and her sessions are always full. This class was booked but I added you. Just arrive early and grab a cushion. I'm sure she will be happy to see you."

Max was waiting anxiously outside the kirtan room. His toes were tapping like he was watching an Irish fiddler playing "Whiskey" in the Jar at a pub in Dublin. He was thirty minutes early and there were already at least thirty people waiting at the door. They stood one behind the other, couples holding hands speaking quietly to each other, strangers introducing themselves and asking about the event they were going to experience.

The crowd looked like any kirtan he would be at in Bali or anywhere else. Young and old alike, people with a peaceful smile, an open heart, and comfortable yoga pants. People were there to sing and be heard, not be seen. In many ways, it was always a bit nostalgic for him. He would see so many young people, young couples, and instantly wish he had known about such things when he was much younger. Those silly thoughts would pass the moment the doors opened and the chanting would begin.

The doors were pushed open by a young staff member of the ashram bringing soft cheers from the crowd. Everyone filed in slowly, grabbed a cushion from the back wall and found a place to sit. There was a slightly elevated deck area where a guitar player, harmonium player and microphones were being set up and tested.

Max placed his cushion against the back wall for extra support. He could sit in Lotus pose for a while, but his knees were not feeling at their strongest from all the recent travel and not keeping up with his yoga practice.

The room filled up in short order. He closed his eyes, took deep breaths. He heard the sounds of a finger tapping a microphone. Then he heard a familiar voice. The voice of a songbird from his backyard in Bali. His eyes opened to see Lea standing at the center of the deck, dressed in white lace. What had been her beautiful long, dark hair was now beautiful short, blonde hair. She was glowing. He could feel her presence the moment their eyes connected. In a gesture that brought tears to his eyes, she smiled at him then tapped her heart.

The room was mostly silent, waiting for Lea to begin the night. She stood front and center. "Welcome everyone. My name is Lea. If this is your first time to Kirtan, I'm so happy you are here. Don't worry about a thing, just have fun. Lyrics are being passed around, and I will call out the matching number so you will know which mantra we will be singing.

"Sing from your heart and forget about your voice. Look around the room, smile at your neighbor and sit in your meditation pose. We will start with three deep breaths, then three long chants of AUM."

The sound of AUM filled the room. It's the sound of the universe, the universal sound repeated around the world in all yoga classes and places of spiritual practice. It's one thing to do it three times at home in your yoga space, but it's altogether a different, higher experience, when it's done in a room with thirty people all chanting at the same time. The vibration of all the voices fills the room. The tone is set.

The vibration could be felt in all four corners of the space. Knees touched the knees of the person sitting next to you. People would turn to look at their neighbor and smile. Hearts were open. Love was happening.

When the last verse was over, the room sat still. People were too high spiritually speaking, to be in a hurry to go anywhere. Lea looked out at the group. "Everyone, please find ten people to hug. Hug the person on your left, on your right, and anyone else you would like to share your energy with."

Max loved this part of the program. His heart was also open and it wasn't unusual for emotional things to come up and out in the form of laughter and tears. He hugged a few people. When he went to hug the woman to his left, he realized it was Jenny from San Diego. She gave him a warm, loving hug that he happily received. "Nice to see you here, Max. Have you done Kirtan before?"

"Hi, Jenny. It's so cool to see you here. And yes, I love Kirtan and go as often as possible in Bali."

"Are you staying here or close by?" Jenny asked.

"I just got a dorm room for three nights and I'll see how it goes at that point. I'm actually a good friend of Lea's and was wondering how I would find her here amongst all these people, and then I saw a sign at the reception area about her Kirtan. So, here I am."

"I love when that happens. Have a great reunion with your friend. If I see you around campus, it would be lovely to have tea or lunch or something. It's always fun to meet someone here from back home."

"Thank you, Jenny. That would be great. Have a great night."

Lea worked her way through the students, exchanging hugs and thanking them for coming. She tapped Max on the shoulder, just as Jenny walked away. "Making new friends already? Lea's smile filled her face. "I am so happy to see you here. I had a strange dream the other night that gave me the feeling I might have a visit from a friend. And here you are."

"You sure it wasn't a phone call from Ingrid?" Max laughed as he said it.

Lea laughed with him then put both her arms around him and held him tight. "Come here, my dear Max. I love you. I can't believe you're in India."

"I'm so happy to see you, Lea. You look so beautiful and happy. Pretty crazy I'm here in India. The one place I never thought I would be."

Lea smiled. "That happens sometimes. When did you get here? Did you come straight to Rishikesh?

"It's only been a week since I left Bali, but it feels like a lifetime. I've had so many incredible experiences." Max was so excited he started to ramble on a bit. "I met a holy man on the train from New Delhi and—"

"Max. I'm sorry. I'd love to hear your story," Lea interrupted. Can we meet again tomorrow? I have a massage in an hour and then I have to catch up on some sleep. I've been teaching every day, plus taking classes and doing the Kirtan."

"Yeah, of course. My god, I was talking nonstop there. I'm excited to see you. I didn't know I would find you on my first stop."

"I'm glad you did. You look really happy and I want to hear about your journey so far in India. Max in India. Sounds like one of your movie titles, eh?" She was smiling as she said it.

"You look really happy, too, Lea. And you sound so beautiful leading the Kirtan. Text me in the morning and we'll figure something out."

"Perfect. Thanks for understanding. I really do want to hear everything." Lea gave Max a kiss on the cheek before she walked away.

Max felt calm, happy inside. He knew he had to put things in their proper perspective. *She said, "I love you,"* he thought, but knew it didn't mean "I love you and want to marry you or live with you again." That's just where her heart space was. *Om Shanti. Moving forward with love for all living things.*

CHAPTER TWENTY-THREE
The Wait is Over

Max was wide awake before the 4 a.m. meditation gong sounded. He woke up to a text message from Lea telling him to meet at a restaurant called Varr Temple Food of India. She said to meet there at 2 p.m. and that it was the best food she's had here. She'd told him he could walk or taxi there.

He was happy and excited with how everything was going. Still, he had eight hours to kill before meeting her for what he hoped would lead to finding the clarity of their relationship and getting to the heart of what they each want from each other and themselves. He knew early morning meditation would be a great way to start his day and clear his mind for whatever happens next.

When he walked into the meditation hall, the difference between his meditation classes at Om Ham and here at Parmarth Niketan hit him immediately. Here, the room was dead silent. The people in the room were sitting in full lotus, hands palm open with index finger tucked under the thumb. No one looked around to see who just walked in.

Couples weren't sitting together holding hands or kissing before class started, nor were they talking about what a great class they'd had and what healer they were going to see in the coming days. No. There was only one reason to walk into this room: focus on yourself, your intentions and the level of consciousness you want to achieve.

When the bell rang for the end of class, Max was happy within himself for barely noticing the sound. He fell into a deep meditation within in moments of sitting down. The irony of it all, he felt so clear, yet he could not remember anything that came up in his mind during the meditation. Maybe that was the good news. In any case, he felt like he had slept for hours. He was wide awake, peaceful, and he could feel the love within him wanting to come out.

The reward for early morning meditation aside from the clear mind, was the gathering of the group for tea and fruit. He wanted to meet some of the others at the ashram and ask questions about their experiences, what made them decide to come, and everything else he could think of. He had good friends in Bali who all spent as much as a year in India letting go of everything else in their life to learn more about what it means to nourish the soul without any distractions. Was *he* up to the task? He was starting to get a feeling he wanted to find out.

As much as he wanted to meet some of the people at the ashram, he wanted to keep his focus on Lea and enjoy the mind space he was in for as long as possible. He went back to his room to take a rest, let the morning truly sink in. First, he wanted to get a nice outfit together for his date with Lea. He hoped it was a date, not a meeting.

He went through his backpack and computer bag to pick out a pendant to wear that would look good over one of his yoga shirts. As he thumbed through his clothes, he felt a small bag or package of sorts. When he pulled it out, he saw a beautiful red velvet pouch tucked between his shorts and t-shirts. Inside it was a small box. He opened it, turned it upside down, and out fell a brilliant black onyx necklace with a small Ganesha figure inside a beautiful pendant that was attached at the center. Taped to the pendant was a note with a red ribbon on the back of it.

He unfolded the small paper and read:

"Dear Max,

Surprise!
We miss you already and hope you will come visit us
with Lea. My father has many pendants and necklaces,
and he told Savitri and me to pick one out for you to give
to Lea, and then hide it in your clothes. We hope you like
our choice.

We all send love.
Rhada, Savitri, Vikram, and Vanya

Max held the beautiful necklace and pendant out in front of him. The pendant was a beautiful earth tone crystal similar to tiger's eye, and inside was a small Ganesha. He would have selected that one for himself if he had the opportunity. It was the perfect gift. He matched it up against a simple V-neck white long sleeve t-shirt just to get an idea of what it would look like on Lea. He felt so much joy. "Thank you, girls and all the Vikram family. Thank you, Universe. I love my life."

Time was completely lost on him. He checked his phone when he stepped out of the shower. It was already one in the afternoon. He decided he would walk to the restaurant, using that time to do as many slow deep breaths as possible. Om Shanti Om, he said to himself as he walked. "I am peace, I am love."

Max walked into the restaurant right on time. It was a minute to two. The short, five-minute walk he was told about ended up being more like a healthy thirty-minute walk. The heat and humidity in India turned his fresh-looking wardrobe into a wilted, wrinkled outfit that looked like it had been worn on a packed train for a few hours. He would have to win Lea over on personality alone.

He looked around the room until a hostess approached. "Hello, sir. May I help you?"

"Ahh, yes. Thank you. I'm meeting a friend here right. She's about my height, short blonde hair, very pretty." As he described Lea, the hostess could hear the excitement grow in his voice with each word.

"Yes, sir. Follow me. There is a beautiful woman as you described sitting at the corner table, just beyond the bar. I'll send someone over with menus. Welcome to Varr Temple Food."

Max followed the directions he was given. He turned the first corner past the bar, and there she was. Lea sat at a table for two facing out towards the restaurant so she could see him coming. Max quickened his pace involuntarily when she waved, reaching her table before her hand came down.

"Hello, my dear Max. Sit, catch your breath. Did you think I was going to run away when I saw you?"

"No, at least not until you finished your meal," he said smiling.

"Ha. True enough," Lea answered. "The food here is worth a little angst if it comes to that."

Max couldn't help but smile. "You know, I wasn't sure how long it would take, if at all, for it to feel like old times sitting with you. It's good to see you, Lea."

The server, a tall, young Indian man, Pavan, as it said on his name tag, came to their table. "Welcome. Would you like a drink to start or are you ready to order?"

Lea looked at Max and asked, "May I order for you?"

"Sure. That sounds great."

Lea looked up at Pavan. "We'll have two besan ladoo and two large iced chai lattes."

"Very well. Good choice. We make the best in all of Rishikesh. It will be right out. Did you want nuts or raisins on top?"

"Both, please. Thank you."

"Besan ladoo? What did you just order for us?"

"Trust me, Max. You'll love it. It's one of the most popular deserts in this part of India. It's a round dessert ball made with gram flour. The flour is roasted with butter, and then sugar is added and it's shaped into balls that are rolled in nuts and raisins. There you go. You will love it."

"Okay, but if I end up locked in my room calling for a doctor, I expect you to sit with me."

"You're forgetting I've been watching you eat for almost two years. You'll be just fine. Now, tell me. Why are you here?"

After their food was delivered, he took a bite of his besan ladoo. His smile betrayed his earlier protests against eating so much sugar and fried dough in one sitting, or even a lifetime. "Boy that's good," he said as he quickly finished the sweet treat. "Let's have a coffee while we talk," Max said as he waved the waiter over and ordered a latte for each of them.

"To answer your question, I'm here because the short time I was in Kintamani I realized how aloof and inattentive I had been towards you and our relationship. I want to fix it."

Lea looked into Max's eyes in the same loving way she always treated him. She reached across the table to take his hand in hers. "Max...You were always kind to me, always supportive and so much more. You're sweet and funny and have a loving heart."

Max removed his hand from Lea's. "Why does it sound like there is a *but* coming."

"Because you can't create passion where it doesn't exist. I've had an amazing few weeks here. The distance helped me put things in perspective without any bitterness or bad feelings."

"I heard you had a little more help with getting that perspective than just the distance."

"Don't be coy, Max. Say what you mean."

"All right. I heard you were back with your old boyfriend, Mobin. Is that true?"

"It's partially true. I did meet up with Mobin. I've known him longer than I've known you and we are good friends. I asked him to join us here so you could meet him. He told me he would be happy to help you find the right programs for you or even a particular teacher. He'll do whatever he can to help you. He's a good man."

"That's… well…. I don't know what that is or what to make of it. It's not what I expected to happen, that's for sure. I came to find you, Lea, and ask you to come home with me."

"Max, you want the illusion of your romantic version of me. That's not who either of us is. It's not who we ever were. I am clear about that now. I wish you every happiness. And if you want to stay here, know you have a friend who loves you."

Max let out a long breath. "Well… I can't or wouldn't blame you for feeling that way. Anyone would. You've given me so many chances. I wish there was a way I could show you that I do have passionate feelings for you." He paused then spoke once again without thinking. "Aside from the obvious, of course."

"Oh Max. You make a joke, but it actually hits at the core of things. Sex is not the obvious. It's a beautiful intricate part of a life two people can share in a loving relationship."

"I'm working so hard to find the answer to why I'm afraid to show love in certain ways. I've always kept my emotions inside. If anyone ever asked me, I always said everything was great. Lea, I want to fix it. Will you give me a chance?"

"I do love you. I know your heart is so sweet and kind. I'm going to talk to my guru here and I promise I will let my heart guide me. I'm going back to Bali tomorrow night. I thought I would want more time here, but with the help of friends, everything becomes clear. When I get back to Bali, after a few days to rest, Ingrid and I are taking a trip to see her parents in Perth."

"How long will you be gone?"

"About a week. Have fun while you're here. I'll see you back in Bali at our home. After that, we'll figure out what's best. Is that good?"

Max got up from his seat. "Thank you, Lea. You look amazing. Beautiful. Happy. And amazing, really. I know I already said that, but I don't know what else to say. I love you and I wish for you to be happy as well in everything you do. Please tell Mobin thank you for me. He's a lucky man."

Lea got up from her seat to hug Max. It was a sweet, loving hug. He felt her true feelings for him, and he felt some relief as well. She said and did things he might not have been able to do or say — and she did it with love. He was truly blessed. *Everything will work out perfectly.*

CHAPTER TWENTY-FOUR

Ashram Munivara

Fleur walked down the stone step path leading to Master Ketut's home and healing center. On each side of the path, the fruits of the Guru's labor and of all the people who came to the ashram to do service was evident, no matter what direction you looked. On one side, the vegetable garden was teeming with varieties of lettuce and greens, on the other there were trees bearing fruits and tea leaves, and coconuts and avocados were in abundance. Everything that was growing at the ashram would eventually end up on a plate at Om Ham's Tulsi Dining room.

At the bottom of the stairs, she noticed the yoga room where she enjoyed a few outdoor classes with proteges of the guru. Just beyond that, was the wooden house she was looking for. In America, there used to be many television commercials for a motel chain called Motel 6. Their tag line was always, "Come on by, we'll leave the light on for you." The same was true at the Master's home. If his porch light was on, he was inside and available to the Indonesian people of Taman Village, and to all those staying at Om Ham and the ashram. His life was dedicated to teaching and healing.

Fleur pushed open the door to enter. Temple incense burned from a corner table filling the room with a sacred aroma. The Guru was sitting on a small throne covered with a white blanket. He was dressed in his ceremonial white sarong and udong. He looked regal.

"Come up and sit. Let's talk." His voice carried to the back of the room in a commanding yet gentle tone.

Fleur walked up and sat, facing him in a simple yoga pose. "Thank you so much for seeing me. I'm filled with questions."

"Ha. Then you must be filled with answers as well. What would you like to know?"

Fleur laughed. He made it sound so simple. like everything was good. He would give her the answers to what she wanted to know. All she had to do was ask the right questions.

She wasn't quite sure where to start. It was one thing for her to think about all the questions in her own mind. It was something else when she was asked to vocalize them to someone. It felt a little threatening to be in such a vulnerable state of mind. She wasn't a religious person, so to speak, but she found comfort enough in the sacred space of the ashram with the Guru.

"Master Ketut, thank you so much. I feel a little uncomfortable about telling you all of my thoughts, because you know everyone I'm talking about. I hope you don't think I'm being petty or mean."

"Fleur. Your thoughts and our time together are for you. There is no judgement, no blame, no one to find fault for anything. Do you understand?"

"Yes. … So, I came here to just get some alone time. I flew out with Ali to spend some time at Max's villa. He invited us to stay while he went to India to find Lea."

"Ahh, Max. He is full of surprises. I was wondering why I had not seen him at yoga this past week."

"Yep. He is on a mission, Master Ketut. I love him, you know, but I don't know if he knows who he really loves or doesn't love."

"You make a good point, Fleur. You know him well and it seems to me that even though you two are always far apart, you are very close. A simple paradox. It's hard for any of us to know what he will do next. He lives his life, and like the rest of us, sometimes a change is needed. So, this is your time. What happened at the villa that created this problem for you?"

"Ali and I were hanging out at the pool. Ingrid came by and we had a nice time. But the next day when I came back from shopping, I found Ali and Ingrid playing in bed together. So, I put a few things in my bag and came here. My emotions were all over the place."

Fleur wasn't sure exactly what to expect. The Guru is known to be direct. He was not known to sit with anyone for an hour like an appointment with a shrink. He felt the energy of the problem, gave his advice and then you're on your own. He's not a hand-holder.

Master Ketut thought for a moment, then started, "You must not let your monkey mind control you. We can all get mad and hurt. It's okay. Give it ten minutes, then push it out of your mind. That's all the time it deserves. No one else can hurt you or change your emotions. Those are up to you. You can decide not to be hurt, not to feel angry. Do you see that?"

"I do. I don't know how though. One minute, I want her to leave, then the next, I want to stay with her."

The Guru stroked his long beard as he thought. "Let me tell you a story of a friend. One day she came home to find someone had damaged her car on purpose. She had it fixed. Then, three days later, it was damaged again in the same exact place. She posted the story on Facebook with photos of her car and asked the questions, 'How does it end? What makes it stop?'

"Many of her friends commented about how horrible the person who did this was, saying he should be in jail, someone should do it to him, and on and on. All this did was keep the negative energy going and getting stronger. All her friends blamed this *horrible* person."

"What did you tell her? How does she make it stop?"

"I told her love and forgiveness stops any negativity. Forgiveness disarms the person who is acting out. We want to know why, but that's impossible to know. You want to know why Ali played with Ingrid?"

"Yes, I would love to know why? Is that bad?" Fleur asked.

"It's human nature to want to know why. But when we understand there is *no knowing*, we can just forgive the person, say I love you, and move on. We invite everything into our lives — good and bad. Does blaming fix anything?"

"No," Fleur answered quietly. Her heart started to open, and the tightness in her face softened.

The Guru continued. "You have a beautiful, good heart. Follow it. If you want to be with Ali, then be with her. This other stuff doesn't matter unless you make it matter."

"Guru, I'm not mad anymore. It made me think. I moved to Los Angeles to find a safe place to be, to escape from my life in Paris. Living there with my mom and sisters was a constant reminder of how sad everyone was. It was too painful for me after my dad died. Being with Ali was fun. Same for being with Max. I love him, but as a dear friend. I love Ali, but I'm beginning to see that I love her in the same way I love Max. They were both friends in my time of need. That's what I am starting to realize. They are not the answer to my happiness."

"No one other than you is the answer. I will say this to you, and that's all. Go be with your family. They miss you and you must put your fear of all those emotions of being with your family away. Go. Sit with them. Be with them. Laugh with them. Celebrate your father and all your lives together. You are a creative, talented woman. Get into what makes you happy, whatever it is. Get into loving and forgiving yourself."

The guru got up from his throne to stand behind Fleur. He put both hands on her head just above the crown chakra. He held them there for about a minute, blessing her with his powerful love and healing energy. "Go. Finish your time here doing yoga and meditation. In three days, you will have all your answers."

That was it. Fleur got up. The expression on her face was that of a woman at peace. If she could maintain it, all would be well.

CHAPTER TWENTY-FIVE

Ali and Fleur

Fleur was back at the reception desk sitting with Eluh. This time it was to say good-bye and see you later. There are no permanent good-byes at Om Ham, generally speaking. The magic there will not hit everyone, but the vast majority of those who stay there feel the Master's energy surrounding them and embodied in the place, so they return whenever possible.

Master Ketut's energy is in the food that comes from the ashram's garden, it's in the swimming pool where he crafted a beautiful blue and white tile infinity symbol on the bottom with soft blue lights that keeps people from wanting to get out once they are in, and it's in the yoga and massage rooms.

Eluh took Fleur's hand and tied a red, white and black string around her wrist. It's a blessing from the Master and Om Ham, signifying love, harmony and unity. She was told to keep it on until it fell off on its own. She had seen these before on Max and Lea, and now she had one for herself.

She enjoyed healing massages, and a sweet, sexy afternoon with a handsome surfer from California. She also got a special blessing from the master. She was ready to see Ali and enjoy some time at the villa.

She also wanted to talk to Max. He would never disappear from her life entirely. So many things came up for her here, it seemed only natural that he did as well. She wanted some Max time.

Back at the Villa

Fleur walked into the villa with a basket of sweets and assorted croissants she'd picked up at Monsieur Spoon. It was always one of Max's favorite places and was well-known for Parisian style chocolate almond croissants and sourdough baguettes. Ali came out of their bedroom as she was putting the goodies on a serving platter in the center of their table.

"Hello, sweet girl. I'm so happy you're here. And wow, what a nice tray of treats! I don't know where to start."

"You should start with me." Fleur smiled in the way she had of being sweet, sexy and funny all at the same time while making a point.

Ali walked up to Fleur and kissed her on the lips. Fleur responded as Ali hoped. She held the kiss, lips open and attached. "Mmmm. You taste like chocolate. It seems you started without me."

Fleur stepped back to look at her friend and lover. Ali was wearing a pajama top that came down to just above her knees, and nothing else. The way the setting sun slowly filtered in through the translucent curtains made her round and full breasts a tantalizing shadow pushing against the white top. She'd known Fleur was coming back but she hadn't known when. The least she could do was show her she was happy and ready for her return.

"You should catch up," Fleur suggested. "I recommend the chocolate almond. I got it especially for you. Then we can both taste the same."

Ali smiled and grabbed at the fluffy croissant and took a big bite. Before she could put it back down on the plate, Fleur moved in and kissed her on the lips. "Much better. I think we should take these into the bedroom."

Ali walked into the bedroom. No way was she going to bring up the situation that separated them. At least not now.

Fleur followed her in. They stopped at the foot of the big bed. The sheets were pulled back, open and inviting. Ali put her hands on Fleur's shoulders and kissed her again.

As they kissed, Ali removed Fleur's t-shirt, then Fleur reached out and pulled Ali's pajama shirt up and over her head. The girls looked at each other with an overdue lust, but neither one moved for a moment.

Fleur dropped her shorts to the floor. "God, you're beautiful."

Ali's eyes devoured Fleur top to bottom. She wasn't sure if it was a yearlong infatuation, but a few days apart set her on fire for her sexy French flower. "Lay down," she said.

Fleur did as she was told, and Ali straddled, one knee on each side of Fleur's naked body, and her sex directly brushing Fleur's. Her hands moved slowly up to Fleur's breasts, massaging, kissing, teasing.

Fleur's head rolled back as her body arched up to meet Ali's kisses, turning her on more and more. The way Fleur's body responded turned Ali on as much as their mutual touching and kissing.

Ali continued her kisses, moving down over Fleur's stomach to the top of her thighs. Fleur's legs opened wider, inviting the attention she desired. Ali's lips moved lower to accept the invitation. Fleur put her hands on Ali's head, holding it over her waiting lips.

The mounting tension was itself a special kind of elixir. She loved the way Ali touched and licked her. It was a big part of what had kept them together for so long. Fleur's hips moved on their own, going up to reach Ali's eager kisses and coming back down in rhythm until she could feel her climax coming.

Their bodies merged. Tongues finding those sacred places, while hands massaged whatever was available. They twisted and rolled over taking turns on top. It didn't matter who was where. The room was filled with the scent of love and sexual pleasure. Their moans filtered out the open French doors into the garden. Even the songbirds stopped to listen.

The Next Morning

Fleur was awake first. She made a cup of tea from the leaves the Guru had given her to help keep her nervous system in check. She took her cup out to the garden to sit in the gazebo. The sun was just rising over the horizon and the prevailing sounds were those of the nearby roosters. It was her favorite time of day.

For whatever reason, she decided to wear one of Max's long-sleeved button-down shirts. It came down just past her waist and left her as close to being naked, her most desired way to be, as she could get while still wearing something. She knew he wouldn't mind since he loved seeing her in his shirts.

She smiled thinking of that and decided to take a selfie to send to him. She sat under one of the palm trees with one knee crossed over the other, and unbuttoned his blue batik shirt to her mid tummy. She knew how sexy this was and looked forward to his reply. She also knew she shouldn't tease him like this if she wanted to leave the sex out of their relationship.

She could still feel her body tingling from the night of pleasure she and Ali shared and she wanted to put it all in perspective while she was alone in nature. Ali would be awake soon, and she knew they had to have a talk about everything.

The Guru had helped her feel strong enough about herself to follow her heart and allow her instincts to tell her what to do. Maybe Ali was feeling some of the same things. Relationships can last a long time when great sex is a constant, but there has to be more in common than that. This is what Fleur decided would be the focus of their conversation.

CHAPTER TWENTY-SIX

Resolutions

Max sat at a table at the Ashram's cafe. He had the gift that Vikram's family had given him and was writing a note to go with it. Writing the note helped him with his feelings for Lea. He wasn't sure how long he would stay in Rishikesh, but with Lea on her way home, he could explore the ashram on his own and get an idea of what a longer stay would be like.

He sipped his morning coffee, hoping that would inspire his decision. His phone chimed with a WhatsApp message. He looked down at the sexy photo of Fleur in his garden. He shook his head, smiling at the same time.

"Something's got your attention. Good morning, Max." Jenny said as she approached him.

"Good morning, Jenny. You're talking. Cool. It's a message from a friend of mine back in Bali. Would you like to join me for coffee?"

"I'm on my way to yoga. *You* should join me. It would be good to experience some of the teachers here before you leave."

"I totally agree. I'll meet you in the classroom. Thank you."

"Wonderful. See you there. Namaste."

Max was interested in getting to know Jenny, as well as making friends at the ashram. There was no reason to rush home. But the message from Fleur gave him an idea. Now that he wasn't going home with Lea, he wanted to ask Fleur if she still felt like coming to India. He decided to find out with a short text.

> Hey, Fleur, are you still interested in visiting India? I can meet you in New Delhi in a couple of days if you are, and we can explore some fun places together. \
>
> I met a really wonderful family and they would be happy to meet you and help us put together a great adventure.
>
> I'm off to yoga. Text me your answer.
>
> Love, Max
>
> Oh yeah, be sure to Google "Toy Train in India".
>
> We should do it.
>
> Okay. Bye."

Meanwhile, Back at Max's Villa in Bali

Ali woke up feeling giddy and concerned all at once. Their bedroom still held the aroma of sex, and her body still felt the endorphin rush of their lusty night together. When she saw Fleur sitting in the garden drinking her tea, she wondered what was going through her mind. Ali thought she looked more contemplative than happy. That usually didn't bode well for a lighthearted conversation.

She walked towards Fleur with a cup of coffee and a croissant. She sat down next to her. "Good morning." She leaned in to kiss Fleur, but Fleur stiffened rather than yielding. "Ahhh," Ali sighed. "So, you want to have that conversation we skipped over yesterday?"

"I do," Fleur answered. "It's complicated and it's not. I loved last night. It reminded me of why I moved from Paris to Los Angeles to be with you."

Ali took a sip of her coffee. "That sounds like one of those compliments a person gives when things are about to change. Do you feel like a change?"

"I do," Fleur replied. "It's never one thing, as you know, and being back here in Bali, being in Max's villa where we first met, has brought up a lot of memories and things that I was ignoring in my own life."

Ali listened to her friend intently. She understood friendships and memories and the personal experiences that come up in life and either shape our next move or give us a reason to stop and think with as much clarity as we can muster. She understood the vulnerable time in Fleur's life when they met. Fleur's father had just died and she was a little lost in life.

Ali could relate. When her best friend and partner Dori passed, she also felt a huge void. She lived in Dori's house, surrounded by photos and memories of all the love and laughter they'd shared. One week she saw her best friend get married, and a short time later she was giving her eulogy.

She felt her eyes redden when she thought of Dori's passing and how it left her feeling so alone. That's when Fleur had entered her life. It wouldn't be unreasonable to consider that maybe, in some way, they'd each confused friendship and love with the safety and love they found in each other's arms. Sweet but complicated co-dependency.

"Ali?"

"I'm here. Sorry. I was listening, taking your words to heart. There's a wise old soul in that young, beautiful body of yours. As you were talking, my life with Dori was flashing before my eyes."

"I'm so sorry about that. It was an emotional time for all of us, in so many ways, and yet it's what connected us all."

Ali agreed. "You, me, Max, Dori. It's like we were all standing together in a circle and the Guru wrapped the red, white and black string around us tying us all together."

"Exactly," Fleur admitted. "Like in that movie *Ticket to Paradise* with George Clooney and Julia Roberts where their daughter gets married to this sexy Balinese boy and at the wedding their family guru and healer tied the string around them."

"Oh, Fleur. You drive me crazy. You're just like Max. Everything is a movie to you both."

"Life is a movie," Fleur answered.

Ali knew it was time to be direct. "So, where is our movie going? Are you riding off into the sunset? Are the final credits rolling?"

Fleur's phone chimed loudly. It was Max's reply to her earlier message. She saw his invitation to come to India and have an adventure with him. "I'm not sure. That's as honest as I can be. I feel like I need to go home, to Paris actually, and live with my family until we all can laugh and enjoy life together again. I feel like I let my mom and sisters down, and I want to fix that. That's what I decided."

"Was that your mom on the phone?"

"No. Actually, it was Max. He invited me to come to India and share an adventure with him before I leave Bali."

"Are you going to do that? Do you want to go to India?"

"Yes. I'll go have an adventure with Max, get the deets on what happened with him and Lea, and then go home to Paris. As I say it out loud, it feels right."

"Can I have a hug?" Ali stood up and looked at her sweet friend and lover for the last year.

Fleur got up and hugged Ali with all her heart. "I love you, Ali. I hope we can be friends forever. Come to Paris whenever you want to escape L.A." Fleur hugged Ali again and kissed her sweetly on the lips.

"I love you too, Fleur. Go pack and have fun with Max. I'm going to stay here for a few more days. Maybe I should go get a dose of the Guru like you did. It seems to have been very good for you."

"Thank you, Ali. It was. He helped me know what was best for me. When he touches you, you feel all this healing going right through all your cells. It's unbelievable."

"Safe travels, Fleur. I'll see you somewhere, yeah?"

"Yes, please. I hope it's in Paris. *Au revoir, mon cher.*"

CHAPTER TWENTY-SEVEN
Yoga

The healing sound of the whole class chanting AUM marked the end of Max's first yoga class in India. He loved it. He loved seeing new people who come from all over the world to experience spirituality in one of its major birthplaces. And foremost, he was so happy that it felt comfortable for him to let go a little bit of his attachment to Bali, Om Ham, and Master Ketut.

"So… what did you think? Was it good for you?" Jenny's bright smile was a comfort. He was happy she took an interest in him and was there to guide him around the ashram. *Karma can be a* good *thing too*, he thought to himself. He had taken so many people on ashram tours for Om Ham. Now he was the guest, a tourist following the lead of a very pretty woman, from his home state of California no less.

"I loved it, Jenny. Thank you for encouraging me. I've been so stuck doing my own practice and staying just with what's familiar for me. I feel like I would like to stay here a while and really study."

"I'm so happy to hear that, Max. Everyone finds what they're looking for if they really want to. Sometimes, we stop short for no other reason than fear."

"That's so true. Are you going to take your wisdom and yoga practice back to San Diego and teach?"

"Soon. I have a few more courses of study. I'm working with a wonderful teacher here, Guru Krishna Dev. He's opened my eyes to more possibilities about living in higher dimensions and higher states of consciousness. I'm meeting him for tea to discuss a particular meditation exercise. Would you like to meet him?"

"I would love to. Now?"

"Yes. Follow me."

Max's phone chimed as they walked. "Do you want to answer that? I can sit for a minute. Guru Dev is just around the corner in the first bungalow."

"Thanks, Jenny. It's my friend Fleur from Bali. I asked her to come visit me here and go on a few adventures, and she said yes. I'll just tell her I'll call in an hour."

Max typed his reply to Fleur, and a minute later, he and Jenny were standing at the door to Jenny's guru. The door opened before she could knock, and Guru Krishna Dev was standing there to greet her. He was tall, wore his long dark hair in a pony tail, and he was an American. Max would learn later that he was from Madison, Wisconsin, and used to go by the name Dave Palmer. That had to be a good story, and it was one he wanted to hear.

"Welcome, sister Jenny. Please come in."

"Sat Nam, Sri Guru Dev. I brought my friend Max with me. He's new here as of two days ago, but he lives in Bali and is familiar with ashram life. And he won't stop talking about kundalini yoga."

"Ha" Guru Dev was laughing already. It didn't take much to get him to smile, but yoga stories were his favorites.

"Welcome, Max. Please come in. I hope you will stay long enough to find the same joy in our yoga practice that you found in Bali."

"Thank you so much, Guru Dev."

Guru Dev escorted Jenny and Max to the small patio behind his bungalow. "Sit. I will bring tea and we will talk."

Max looked into Jenny's eyes. He was high from class and felt the great energy and vibrations of the huge ashram, and the power from Guru Dev now as well. "Thank you, Jenny. I'm so happy to be here with you. I get the feeling Guru Dev has an interesting story."

"He sure does. He's like a guy you would meet at the beach surfing or playing volleyball — one you wouldn't suspect had a spiritual connection to the source. He's become a great mentor for me."

"I get that. For me, it's Master Ketut in Bali, but it's very easy to feel the grace and elevated energy of Guru Dev. I would definitely like to sit and talk with him."

"He would love that. You're both around the same age, but most of *his* life was here in India. I'll let him tell you the story, but both his parents died within weeks of each other. He was only eight and ended up living with his uncle."

"That's pretty intense. Who knows what could happen to anyone emotionally, let alone a child of eight."

"For sure. He ended up with his uncle who was transferred to New Delhi. By the time Dev was twelve, he was living near the ashram right here. He enrolled in classes and found his calling."

Jenny left Max to take that all in. It was time for her session with her friend. "I'll be out in about an hour. You're welcome to hang out and wait, or leave your number and Sri Guru Dev will call you if you'd like to sit with him."

"That's great. I would like that. Hey…before you leave, can I ask you something?"

"Sure, Max. What is it?"

"Well, I've heard people at Om Ham refer to our guru as Sri guru at times, and now I hear you use that same greeting. What does it really mean?"

"It's showing reverence in the higher sense of a greeting to an enlightened or holy man. In the most basic way it can be interpreted as similar to addressing someone as 'Mr. So-and-so.' Does that help?"

"A little, I guess. I don't hear it very often. I've heard people talking at the ashram about greeting the guru in that way, but I don't feel comfortable with it. I can't explain it other than I don't put people on pedestals."

"That's all right, Max. I like to use a very simple analogy when asked about it. Do you call a medical professional, doctor?"

"I sure do. Hmmm. Thank you. Really good answer. That's a guru answer."

Jenny blushed a bit with her smile. "No problem. I doubt any doctor who is truly comfortable with himself and not into his ego would really care. If we learn to treat all people with love and kindness, I think we've done good."

"It's funny, Jenny. I think Jesus Christ could appear out of thin air right in front of me and I would have no desire to drop to the ground to kiss his feet. But I would love to sit and talk to him."

"You're a funny guy, Max. I'd love to be a fly on the wall for that conversation."

"I'm so happy to meet you, Jenny. I don't have many people I can talk to about spiritual things and the aspects of living a spiritual life that are still a problem for me. Thank you."

"I'm happy to meet you too, Max. If you stay here, I hope we can become friends. If not here, I'll come visit your ashram in Bali and *you* can be the tour guide. How's that?"

"It's absolutely perfect. Can we exchange contacts?"

"I would love to."

Jenny tapped her phone to his to do to the contact exchange.

"I'll see you later, Jenny. I'm going to have a bite to eat and help my friend with her reservations to get here."

"Om Shanti, Max. See you."

Max checked over his text to Fleur before sending it. He wanted to make sure she felt free to come and go as she pleased, with no strings attached. He would always have feelings for her and they shared something very special the first time they met. Dori understood it, and so did Lea. Sometimes they each wondered why he wasn't with her.

The answering text came quickly. Fleur would get a flight to New Delhi in a few days. He arranged to meet her at the airport and to do a few more classes at the Parmarth Niketan.

Max's toes were tapping again — this time out of pure joy and the inability to sit still. He was excited to see Fleur and now he had some real questions he could talk to Guru Dev about. A different voice would be a good thing.

A Little Later with Guru Dev

Max sat in easy pose opposite Guru Dev at the fountain in his back yard. "So, Max, tell me what finally brought you to India after all the years in Bali and exploring yoga and mediation? Jenny told me that you came here to see your girlfriend, Lea, and talk to her about your life together. She's an amazing woman, let me just say. I know that whatever is best for you two will work itself out."

"That's probably ninety percent of it. Every time I'm at an event like a Kirtan or Tibetan Bowl mediation I hear people talking about their experiences in India. So many times, I hear someone say 'to really find your true spirituality, you have to go to India.' Do you believe that?"

"Spirituality is a personal journey for each one of us. Mine is very different from yours, yours is very different from Lea's, and so on. You can find your truest aspirations anywhere in the world. You might meet someone on a bus or walking a canyon trail in San Diego who says words that are like a bright light into your spiritual universe. India is a truly spiritual place and a holy center of the universe, but if spirituality only happened here, where would we be as a planet?"

"I agree. I feel the same. That's why I never felt I had to come to India to learn how to meditate, find my higher self and be someone who contributes to losing the duality in the world that separates us all. I love the concept but have a hard time putting it to work."

"You're an interesting guy, Max. We all have that problem. Gurus and yogis just starting out on their path. What is it about your relationship with Lea that pushed you to make this trip?"

"That's a question I have been trying to answer for a few months now, and one that's come up between us for the last year. We actually talked yesterday. We were able to laugh and share our observations for going forward and we each realized we could do that, but the things that we aren't happy with now would still be there. So, we decided to trust in our great friendship and leave it at that, being thankful for trusting each other and caring for each other."

"A true friend you can count on is a good thing in life, Max. It sounds like you both understand that is worth more than trying to be what you're not. So, what's next for you? Do you think you would like to study here for six months or a year and test that theory about finding spirituality in India?"

"Maybe. I have a dear friend coming to visit me. We're going to do some trekking and share in some fun adventures. We have feelings for each other, but we put them aside due to circumstances. Kind of like parents staying together for the sake of the kids. Now, I think we might be able to find out what our potential could be."

"Trust yourself, don't be afraid of love and have a great time. I'll see you when you return."

"If I come back, this is where I will be," Max replied.

Guru Dev got up to shake Max's hand and give him a hug. He was glowing and full of light. Max could feel his energy when they hugged and he would swear today that he saw visions of Fleur and Satya all at once. "Remember, Max. There is only one God, one Guru. He is inside you. Go find him."

CHAPTER TWENTY-EIGHT

Max and Fleur in India

Max fidgeted with his phone like an 8th grader at the championship spelling bee waiting for his next word. To put it mildly, he was excited to see Fleur. He was happy with the extra few days in Rishikesh at the Ashram. It gave him a better insight into what he would experience if he decided to come back and explore his spiritual journey with new teachers. And he had made a new friend in Jenny. She was from San Diego. A place he'd called home for many years. It's nice to meet someone from your home area. It was the same kind of connection that started his relationship with Dori. *Something to think about,* he mused.

But that was for later. He and Lea had a great talk about their needs and he was able to express himself freely. Lea was gone and on her way to Perth with Ingrid. They would reconnect back at their home in Bali in week or so. Now, he could share some fun time with Fleur. They were each living their own lives. She had Mobin and the ashram, and he had Fleur.

He checked his phone for any delays while he stood at the last exit gate Fleur would have to walk through before she was free to move about. Everything was on time.

Just like inside the Bali airport in Denpasar, there was a sea of humanity she would have to wade through to find him. He hoped she would notice the sign he was holding. It didn't have her name on it, instead the expression she used so often that always made him laugh graced the sign in large hand-printed black Magic Marker: *"Can you imagine?"* He hoped she would see it and know it was for her. It was their own inside joke. A true sign they shared something special.

Finally, his phone buzzed. He pulled it from his pocket.

I'm here. Find me.

Short and sweet, just like Fleur. He held his sign higher and waved it around in all directions. Before another worrisome thought could enter his mind, he heard his name. "Max…*Ou êtes vous? Max. Je suis ici.* I am here."

There she was, her big smile partly hidden under her straw sunhat. She wore khaki shorts with pockets, an Om Ham t-shirt, and her trademark extra-large man's button-down shirt over it. Unbuttoned of course. It was almost exactly how she looked the day they first met.

Max laughed to himself. She looked beautiful that day and every day. She always looked beautiful to him. "Fleur," he called out. Before another word was spoken, she rushed into his arms for a hug and a kiss.

"Maxie, my sweet *mon ami.* Thank you, thank you!"

"Hello, my sweet Fleur. It's so great to see you here. I can't believe it, really. I'm excited to share India with you."

Fleur had a medium-sized backpack over her shoulders and a smaller hand-held duffel that also had rollers.

"I see you have the warm weather covered. Any chance you brought something for the cold air of the mountains and Kathmandu?"

"Oui, oui, yes. There is a chance," she said smiling.

"Whew. That's good." Max breathed a sigh of relief. It was only momentary.

"But I didn't," she quickly added. "Can we go shopping here?" Her eyes were smiling with the rest of her face.

"Ahhh. My sweet Fleur. What was I thinking? Let's get outta here. There has to be a designer shop somewhere."

Max and Fleur held hands walking out of the Indira Gandhi Airport. The age difference between them didn't matter when they first met over two years earlier, and it didn't matter now. They each knew it would never matter.

When they reached the transport area, a big black and gray Mercedes Maybach pulled up to them. Fleur's eyes opened wide. "What's this?" Before Max could answer, Devi Patel, dressed in his official chauffeur's uniform, stepped out to open the back door of the limousine. "Mr. Max. Your car is here," he said.

His smile was big and his Indian dialect was strong and commanding. "Please, get in. I will take you to your hotel."

"Thank you, Devi. This is my friend, Fleur. She's the one I was telling you about. She had no idea you were coming."

"So happy to surprise you. Welcome, Ms. Fleur."

Devi greeted Max with a warm handshake. "I have been instructed to take to you to a grand hotel and drop you off. I will pick you up in the morning at ten o'clock sharp. Master Vikram has a day planned for you."

"Thank you, Devi. It feels good to see you and I'm excited to see Vikram and the girls."

"Yes, Mr. Max. The girls are excited to see you as well. Rhada is fixing your room. And of course, Ms. Fleur will have her own suite. Shall we go?"

"Yes, please," Fleur replied. "I definitely need a shower and a nap before anything. Well, maybe some food would be nice too. I'm not sure if am more tired or more hungry."

Devi and Max laughed. "Vanya prepared some Indian sweets and snacks. They're in the car. Enjoy," he said as Fleur and Max were escorted into the back seat.

Devi took the long way through some of the villages, pointing out what he knew of life in New Delhi, and India as a whole, for that matter. Max and Fleur talked and devoured the homemade dosas of chocolate and strawberry, and used the plate of naan bread to dip into the incredible spinach curry Savitri had made for them. It was a perfect pairing. Max loved spicy foods any time of day, and Fleur felt the same about sweets.

"We're here, sir."

Max and Fleur looked up to see this gorgeous hotel, Leela Palaces. "Devi. Where are we?"

"Master Vikram wanted you and your guest to have a wonderful experience. This hotel is also close to his home, so it will be easy for us to come to get you in the morning."

"It looks like a mini Taj Mahal with all the gold domes. I wasn't expecting anything this fancy."

"Not to worry about anything, sir. Master Vikram has many friends in his neighborhood. A few years ago, he helped the owner of this hotel get all the permits and licenses. The owner was only too happy for the opportunity to do a favor for him in return. Your suite is 'on the house,' as you say. So, enjoy. Swim, use the spa, whatever you want. There is also a very nice gift shop. Have fun."

Devi took the few bags they had and handed them off to the hotel's concierge. "This man will take you to the registration desk and get you up to your suite. I hear you will have a most fantastic view for the sunset tonight."

"Mr. Devi. Thank you for everything. This is my very first day in India, and it's already so exciting. Is it okay to hug you?"

Devi smiled and accepted her offer. *Good move,* Max thought to himself.

The hotel concierge opened the door for Max and Fleur to welcome them into the hotel. The lobby was as opulent as one could imagine. There was a huge silver chandelier hanging from the ceiling. Not far from the lobby bar, a tall fountain spouted short bursts of water that changed colors every minute. It was breathtaking.

The concierge walked ahead of them to the front desk. They got their keys to the room along with gift cards they could use for the spa and pool if they desired. One card was also good for two welcome drinks in the hotel lobby. Impressive.

A tall Indian Bellman in full uniform took the hand cart with their luggage. "I can take your things up to you room if you would like to have a welcome drink at the bar."

Max looked at Fleur. She shook her head no, which was fine with him. "No, thank you. But if you don't mind, I'll take the key to the room and the cart. We'll leave it outside the door."

"That will be fine, sir. Anything you would like. If there is anything else we can help you with, just press the concierge tab on your room phone."

Max reached into his pocket and pulled out some tip money for the bellman. "Thank you, sir. Top floor, turn to the right when you exit the elevator. Room 1420."

A minute later Max and Fleur walked into their room. It was stunning. She was so moved by the view, she walked directly to the sliding glass doors leading to the terrace. "Max, are you looking at this? You can see the whole city from here."

"I will in a minute," he called from the bathroom. "Sorry. I had to go… you know." He was laughing at his own humor but when he walked out of the bathroom, he stood next to Fleur in equal amazement.

Out in the distance was a vast view of New Delhi. Tall, modern buildings, grassy fields, the famous New Delhi Gate which is a landmark similar to America's Tomb of the Unknown Soldier, and of course, the landscaped grounds of the hotel.

As they looked out, Max recounted a story Devi told him about the city. "You know, this used to be a part of a mountain range, Aravali. But with time, weather and natural erosion there's not much left. The remaining area is called the Delhi Ridge. Due to all of the smog in the city, the nickname for the Delhi Ridge has now become the "Lungs of Delhi.""

"That sounds gross," Fleur said.

"Hey. Be happy you didn't get a rickshaw ride with me. Although I might not have minded plucking splinters from that cute bottom of yours."

"In your dreams, Maxie boy. I'm going to shower. Okay?"

"Yep."

"For a long time," she added. It had already been a long day and the idea of doing anything else was long gone.

"Take your time. I'll do the same when you're done."

Max enjoyed his shower while Fleur napped on their king-sized bed for a minute. When he finished, he grabbed one of the guest robes from the closet and went out to take in the sunset view from the terrace. It was spectacular and went as far as the eyes could see.

Fleur came out in her robe to join him. She held it to her face relishing the softness. "Can you believe these robes? I could wear this all day."

He was sitting on a lounge chair, wearing the other robe. "Yes, ma'am. First class all the way."

"What's that you're drinking?" Fleur asked.

He was holding a fancy shot glass filled with an orange colored mixture of alcoholic ingredients. "It's a famous Indian rice liqueur. You want one? It's really good. The mini bar is stocked full."

They sat together talking until the sun was down. Max loved her French accent. He could listen to her talk all night. And when she laughed, he laughed with her. Before they knew it, the only light was from the surrounding buildings and the hotel.

A few empty liqueur glasses covered the snack trays, along with the half-eaten salads and fries they ordered up to their room. Airports and immigration lines can sap anyone's energy, regardless of age. Before he could ask Fleur another question, he noticed her eyes were closing. He gave her a gentle nudge. "Shall we go to bed?"

"Yes. Sorry, I didn't think I would be this tired."

"It's okay," Max agreed.

"Bali to India is a long ride. We could both use a good night's sleep."

"I want to talk to you about so much."

"Can we cuddle tonight and talk in the morning?" Fleur asked.

"That sounds so good. It's been way too long since I've had a Fleur snuggle."

Max and Fleur found their comfort zone quickly. The Egyptian cotton sheets and fluffy pillows were a slice of heaven. For Max, it felt like their romantic weekend in Kintamani just happened a minute ago, not like the two years it really was.

That's how it is with the true connections in your life. It felt that way for Fleur as well.

Their robes were off, laid on each side of the bed. Their chemistry and feelings for each other took over almost immediately as their tired, naked bodies rested against each other. Fleur kissed him on the lips gently, to say good night. Max returned her kisses. She wasn't surprised. When he turned her on her stomach to massage her shoulders and back, it felt too good for her to ask him to stop. Sleep could wait a little longer.

Her body softened to his touch. He massaged her with long deep strokes, finding the spots that needed attention and working deep into her muscles. She let out slight whimpers of pleasure as she exhaled.

Fleur could feel the sensations building inside her. This was turning into more than the cuddle she bargained for, but she felt helpless to stop it. She loved the pleasures of the flesh. It was embedded in her nature and she was not shy or self-conscious about it.

But this was not a tryst with a stranger at the Om Ham pool. This was her dear friend she had not seen in a while. He was her handsome American rescuer when they first met, and she felt as close to him as anyone in her life, other than her father. All the more reason to hold back until they could talk without their physical attraction getting in the middle of it all. She hoped.

Max could sense a little hesitation in her when his hands moved lower between her legs to massage her thighs and bum. *She has the best bum.* He massaged it like he was kneading dough for the king's bakery.

When he stopped for a moment, it was the perfect moment Fleur needed. She turned over on her back and touched his lips with her fingers. "Max, will you just hold me until I'm sleeping?"

Max was turned on, but relieved as well. He cared for her so much. This was too fast and it was only repeating their same pattern. "I would love to." He kissed her fingers one at a time and moved his arms around her. Fleur let her head rest easy on his chest while his right arm rested against her hips. Her body felt warm against his. They relaxed into each other, breathing slower and slower. In a moment, they were lying together in spooning position, front to back with Max facing front against her. They fell into a deep, happy sleep.

The next morning

Max woke up first. He tried to pull his right arm from under Fleur's head without waking her. He had to, it was almost numb. When he achieved this mission, he sat up in their gigantic king-sized bed then leaned back against a handful of soft, white down pillows.

He could not take his eyes off the incredibly beautiful, sweet woman lying next to him. The soft sheets rested on her breasts, not fully covering them as they moved up and down with her breathing. He always marveled at her beauty, because in all the time he had known her, his real attraction was to her heart and soul.

Max felt relieved that they didn't have sex. Not because he didn't want to, but because he wanted to know if he could be with her *without* having sex. He was so happy about their night together. He'd never felt so free within himself while lying naked with a woman he cared for.

For whatever reason, he could feel a few tears trickle down his cheeks. His heart felt so open he wanted to scream out, "I love you!" The way he felt right now, he loved everyone. It was during moments like this that he could understand how higher consciousness people felt every day. That's what he wanted for himself.

Fleur's eyes opened before he noticed she was awake. She saw him using his thumb and fingers to rub his eyes and wipe away the tears. She sat up next to him, sharing the pillows. "Max, are you okay?"

"Yes. I am just so happy. How are you? Did you sleep well all night?"

"Unbelievable. I don't even remember dreaming."

"Me either," he said as he looked into her eyes. "I was listening to you breathe. I could feel myself against you. Then I fell into a very deep sleep.

"I know what you mean," Fleur assured him. "I felt you all night, even when I was sleeping. It became dream-like. It felt good. You feel good, Max." She reached from under the covers to rub his chest.

"Were you crying just now?" she asked with concern.

"Not really crying. My emotions go the better of me. My heart felt so open and filled with love. I feel so good."

Fleur rubbed his chest in soothing strokes under the covers next to him. After a minute, her hand dipped a little below his waist. She stopped to feel his blood rushing. She could feel the heat in her hands. She smiled at him with a twinkle in her eyes. "Do you feel good enough to give me the rest of my massage?"

She didn't need a verbal answer, but he gave her one anyway. "I love touching you, Fleur. We will still be the same after, right? I don't ever want to lose you as my friend."

"You will never lose me as your friend. I love you, Max. I don't want to marry you, but I love you. This is the same for you, yes?"

"Yes," he said laughing. "How did you get so smart?"

"Shhh. Quiet. No more questions."

Max changed his position when she rolled over on her tummy. He straddled her back gently. He reached up to her neck with both hands, so he could glide back down, smoothly with pressure in all the right places. After a few trips up and down, his hands rested between her legs. He could feel the heat of her inner thighs.

He started to kiss down her back then below her hips to where his hands were touching her. She could feel the heat with every move. He wanted to kiss her everywhere, but before his lips could move lover, she reached between his legs. It wasn't what she wanted. He was morning hard, and she wanted him inside her. They fit like vanilla ice cream on hot apple pie or two doves cooing on an olive tree branch.

He moved slowly, letting their bodies find the rhythm they wanted. Slower, faster, then slower again. There was no consciousness of time, only each moment of ecstasy.

Fleur's legs quivered then squeezed him tightly inside her as they both let go. Max stayed on top of her for a moment until their breathing calmed down and her legs opened enough for him to ease off of her. He rolled over next to her letting out a long sigh.

Breakfast at the Leela Palaces

Max and Fleur picked a quiet table in the rear of the breakfast room. They had large juice glasses filled with an orange/mango mixture and topped with mint leaves. It was unusually quiet between them, until Max broke the silence. "Fleur, are we good? We're each in the beginning of some changes in our life. One thing I feel so good about is that I am so happy to be with you. Do you mind sharing your thoughts, feelings, or whatever you are comfortable with?"

"I feel the same, Max. I'm very happy to be with you now, and I'm happy whenever I'm with you. For whatever reason, we seem to come together when we each need a good friend."

Max was still searching for something. "This is more than what good friends do, isn't it?"

"What's more, what's less? You think too much sometimes. Don't make anything of it or we can lose it".

"You're right. I should shut up. It's stupid to try to figure it out. I guess, in some ways I feel weird because the sex I have with Lea is not this free...I'm sorry if I shouldn't say that to you."

"It's okay, Max. We fuck. We kiss, we laugh, we play and then we are apart. With Lea, you are trying too hard to know if you want to live with her or marry her or whatever. You make love, but you don't fuck. If you don't feel free to fuck her then maybe she is not the one for you.

"I thought you were going to shut up." Max started laughing. It felt like he just went through therapy. "You're one hundred percent right. I just couldn't say it the way you said it. Right to the point and so true."

"I could say the same about being with Ali. We are mostly friends who enjoyed some fun sex together. It's not the worst thing, is it?

"You're so funny. No. It's not the worst thing. Shall we get our breakfast and begin our adventure?"

Fleur was happy to move off topic. "Yes, please. But also, can we not try to figure it out? Master Ketut told me our problem is we are always asking why. Always trying to figure things out. Let's go on our adventure, which you still haven't told me about."

"All right, my dear Fleur. Here it is. I called my friend Vikram. Devi is picking us up in an hour. We're going to his house to meet the family, hang out, and spend the night. In the morning, we are going shopping and relaxing. Then, the next day, we are taking a short flight to one of the most beautiful cities in India."

"Where? Which one?"

"You'll find out soon enough. For now, let's check out that buffet.

Fleur got up to get something to eat, and Max followed right behind her. When they were waiting at the tray filled with vegetable samosas, Fleur kissed him on the cheek. "It sounds like a great adventure, Max. I'm happy you're in my life. Don't ever leave." She kissed him again, then filled her plate.

CHAPTER TWENTY-NINE

A Day with Vikram

Max and Fleur waited at the entrance of the Leela Palaces. At exactly 10 a.m., as promised, the beautiful black and silver Mercedes Maybach pulled into the circular driveway. This time, however, when the driver's door opened, it was Vikram who stepped out. He was in a beautiful white and gold robe that came down to his ankles. "Good morning. Are you ready for a fun day? The girls and Vanya are excited to see you."

"Good morning. What a great surprise. Vikram, this is my friend, Fleur." Max said as he and Fleur walked up to the car.

"Welcome to India, Fleur. Is this also your first visit?"

"Yes, it is. Max has told me so much about you. How you met on the train and your beautiful home. And meeting Devi. Thank you so much for this."

"You are most welcome. Now, Please. Let's go." Vikram's big smile took over his face as he opened the back doors to his car. "I do not like to be late when my wife is expecting me."

The drive to Vikram's house was fast and easy. The morning air was clear after a night of thunderstorms and the day looked promising. Devi was standing in the driveway when they pulled up. He opened the back doors for Max and Fleur, as Vikram got out of the driver's seat.

Fleur had no idea of the beautiful home they were walking into. "This is so nice. It looks like we could be in the heart of Beverly Hills or the suburbs of Paris. It's just gorgeous."

Vikram appreciated the joy in Fleur's words. "Come inside. My family is waiting." They all walked in. In the hallway, Vanya, Rhada, Savitri were all standing to greet them.

"Hi, Max. It's great to see you again. We're all going shopping together. Is that okay?" Savitri was so excited to see Max. She also wanted to hear about his romantic search for his girlfriend.

"That sounds perfect, Savitri. This is my good friend, Fleur. She's from Paris, France, and she loves shopping."

Fleur hit Max's arm in a playful manner. "Nice to meet you all. And don't let him fool you, he loves to shop too. You should see his closet at home." The girls laughed, having fun with their new guest.

Vanya held out her hand to greet Fleur, and her daughters did the same. Rhada was excited that Fleur was from Paris. "Fleur, that's such a beautiful name. I want to go to Paris one day. Is it as romantic as in the movies?"

"It really is," Fleur answered. "I think it is even more romantic. I love Paris. In French I would say, *j'adore Paris.*" Fleur gave the words and extra heavy French pronunciation. The girls laughed then repeated in their best effort to sound French.

"*Tres bon,* girls. Would you like to learn a few more words?"

"Mom, can we? Savitri was excited to have another guest in their home who was from somewhere far away.

"Girls, that is up to Fleur. She is our guest," Vanya reminded them. "Let's go to the patio before it gets too hot."

Vanya led the way to the patio with the girls right behind her. Vikram stayed back to walk with Max. "So, Max. This is not the woman you were looking for, Lea? What happened?"

"I did find Lea. We talked and had lunch and we both found ourselves at ease with being good friends who were comforting each other and good to each other. It just was not the romantic connection I hoped for, but as is often the case with me, the women in my life know better than I do."

"You are not alone in that, my friend. Vanya is the boss around here. Don't believe otherwise."

Max was relieved. "I'm glad you understand. I'll see Lea again in Bali."

"And Fleur? I get the feeling there is romance with her."

"Yes. We have a lot of passion together. We laugh and play. We're able to talk about anything and be honest with each other. And, the sex we have is so good. It's honest and fun. Does that make any sense?"

Vikram put his hand on Max's shoulder. "I get a very good feeling seeing you with her. When you stand next to her you look together. Sex is a miracle of God. It brings true joy when you have found someone special in your life. I like her."

"Thank you, Vikram, I do to."

Vanya and the girls were chatting like old friends. The girls were asking Fleur to say things in French, then trying to repeat in the same way. Vikram and Max joined them. "Fleur, you are being very kind. Are my girls torturing you yet?"

"Father!" Rhada exclaimed.

Fleur came to their rescue. "It's no problem. Your girls are sweet and it's fun for me. Rhada said we're going shopping? Is that okay for you?"

"It's our day to have fun. Rhada loves this market called GK1. It's very high end and a renowned shopping haven for the elite. It's very diverse. You will find what you need for your adventure to the mountains."

Fleur's eyes lit up. "We're going to the mountains, Max?"

"Yes. Cat's out of the bag. You may as well know now so you know what to buy. We're going on the Toy Train in Shimla."

Devi appeared on the patio. "The car is ready, sir."

Vikram put his arm around his youngest daughter, Rhada. "All right. Let's go. Everybody in."

Shopping at GK1

Shopping was a blast. Vanya and the girls went in one direction, and Vikram and Max the other. The GK Market was a giant conglomeration of luxury items for any person or occasion. Window shopping alone could take a few days.

The girls got mani/pedis. They tried on outfits from hats to shoes and everything in between. Savitri and Rhada had the best time with Fleur. They checked out summer dresses, shorts, and sunglasses, playing with different looks.

Rhada, the fashionista of the two, helped Fleur find a gorgeous white ski jacket and very cool funny mittens for the mountains. She looked like a model for a snowboarding company.

Vikram led Max to where he bought his robes and ceremonial clothing. There was also a fine collection of yoga shirts that Max was happy to sort through. He picked a couple he liked and a sarong he could wear to see Master Ketut back at Om Ham. Finally, he found a thermal long-sleeved t-shirt he could wear under his windbreaker for the colder weather in the mountains.

They topped off their day with fun coffee drinks at the Blue Tokai Coffee Roasters. By the time they reached Vikram's house, it was a full day of fun for everyone. Fleur received a lifetime invitation from the two girls and an invitation to their weddings whenever that would be.

Vikram led Max into his library. It had the look of a professor's office with oversized leather chairs, long leather sofas ideal for naps, and hundreds of books lining the shelves.

"Is this your sanctuary?" Max asked.

"You could say that. I like to look out into the garden, sit and read, or just sip some of Vanya's teas here. It's very relaxing."

"It feels like a safe space to let go of anything that might be bothering you."

"It is that indeed, Max. If you don't mind me saying so, you seem very much at ease with Fleur. Much more at ease than when you were here last week on your own."

"That's a fair observation. When I'm with her, she gives me a feeling of confidence and security that I'm sometimes lacking. She looks up to me, and accepts me for who I am. We don't argue about anything. I feel the same about her. I think she's so smart and funny and full of love for all the people in her life."

"My girls love her. It's easy to see she has a beautiful heart and kindness within her."

"Thank you, Vikram. I know we have a special connection. We're both trying to figure out exactly what it is."

"Don't try too hard. It will take care of itself. Love is like all other things in that sense. The less we mess with it, the better off we are."

The sun dropped behind the night sky as the men chatted. Vikram's house was dotted with solar lights hidden in the bushes and walkways, making the entrance to his home and garden look like something out of a fairytale.

Vanya called out from the kitchen. "Vikram? Dinner is being served. Please come in with Max and bring the girls from the den."

Max wasn't used to dinner much past five or six in the afternoon, but when he saw the table settings Vanya put out, he knew he was in for something special. He sat next to Fleur, with Rhada one side of her and Savitri on the other. Vanya and Vikram sat at the ends of their table. It was a dinner fit for a royal family. The dhal and the masala dishes were the best he ever tasted. Fleur was still laughing and talking in French to the two girls and Vanya, while he and Vikram talked about his upcoming trip with Fleur that would start the next morning.

Rhada took Fleur to her room. She gave her the room Max had on his visit so she could enjoy the rainforest shower and stone tub. Savitri took Max to a different room that was no less amazing. "Is Fleur your girlfriend?" she asked.

"It's hard to say how we would describe our relationship. I love her and I like her very much. I think she feels the same about me."

"She does. We asked. I hope you stay with each other and come back to visit us."

"Thank you, Savitri. Your family is very special to me, and now to Fleur as well. I will stay in touch with your dad. Sweet dreams. See you in the morning."

"Sweet dreams to you, Max."

CHAPTER THIRTY

The Road to Shimla

It was hard to say goodbye to the Vikram family for Max and Fleur. They were so kind and generous and visiting them also gave them a little cover from just being with each other nonstop. Without each other knowing it, when they were all shopping, they had each bought little thank you gifts, both hosts and guests. They exchanged them over breakfast and shared their appreciation. Max invited everyone to his villa in Bali with sincere hopes they would take him up on his offer.

Devi was up early. He enjoyed using Vikram's power washer to get the car clean and maintain it so it looked like new. He knew Max and Fleur would be leaving soon and he wanted everything to be just right.

He put their backpacks in the trunk, then parked in the driveway to wait for them. It wasn't long before they walked out with the whole family to say their final goodbyes. Max shared a quick hug with Vikram and Vanya and that was that. They got settled in the spacious backseat, turning back to wave to their new friends as Devi drove away. They were off to Indira Gandhi International Airport.

It was a short flight to Shimla, barely one hour. By the time Fleur finished her orange juice, the plane was landing. The airport in Shimla was much smaller than in Delhi, more like a small city in the United States, which made it much easier to navigate, especially for newcomers. Because it was a domestic flight, there was no immigration. They had their bags with them, so all they had to do was grab a taxi.

Fleur seemed a bit restless. She'd had a very busy week with Max and a busy and stressful week in Bali leading up to where they were standing. It was a lot.

Thankfully, Max was aware of it. After a little more than two years, he knew her enough to know when she needed a little space of her own.

"Fleur, I have a great day and night planned. We're going to a fabulous hotel on the ridge with mountain views, there will be a spa waiting for you and a massage if you like. From a professional," he added with a smile.

"Thank you, Max." She learned from Max the value of letting out some deep breaths now and then, and proceeded to let out a big one.

"Good one," he teased.

"I'm sorry. I think a lot of things are catching up with me all at the same time. Those girls are sweet, but, they are a handful. I'm tired."

"I can only imagine, as someone I know might say. I threw you into a lot of action. It's not easy being a guest. You were amazing with the two girls and Vikram told me how much they adore you. Today is for you, okay? You tell me what sounds good, and we'll do it."

Fleur let her big Fleur smile come back. "Okay. I can do that."

Max flagged down a taxi, and after some winding roads and short rides through the few small business districts, they were at the Radisson Hotel of Shimla. It was high on the ridge with great views of the Himalayan Mountains.

This was the first time Fleur saw cows grazing down the main streets in a town. They were considered a blessing to the people who lived there. If they didn't find some grass or water, the townspeople would bring it to them like room service.

He told Fleur the little bit that he knew about Shimla, but most of all, that it's the home to one end of the iconic UNESCO World Heritage Site Railway, The Toy Train. The other end is in the city of Kalka. The city itself was one of the cleaner cities in all of India and had a bit of a European flair. That was especially appealing to Fleur. She was not one who was going to be standing in line to wade in the Ganges.

"So, we're taking this Toy Train ride?"

"We sure are. That's why we needed the winter clothes. We'll need them tonight if you're up for going somewhere nice for dinner. If not, we'll need them in the morning. Tomorrow is wide open. We can spend the day exploring the city and we can do the train the day after. Whatever you want."

"That sounds fun. Can we check in now?"

"Yep. Let's go do it. I'm excited to see the Himalayan Mountains up close."

"Me too, Max. This is so nice and it's just about us, finally."

"All righty. We'll go check in. After we drop our bags, I'll go arrange a tour guide for the day while you go spa yourself. How's that?"

Fleur gave Max a quick kiss on the cheek. "It's perfect."

While Fleur was at the spa, Max reached into his backpack for the gift he'd bought for her at the big market. It was a silver charm that said "Om Shanti" on one side and "Fleur" on the other. He had it done at the shop Vikram took him to and was excited for her to find it under her pillow.

He grabbed a bottled water from the room's mini bar and sat outside on the small balcony to write a note to put in the jewelry box.

Dear Fleur,

*Thank you for being such a great friend. Ever since the day
we met at the Black Lava Hostel in Kintamani you have
held a special place in my heart."*

Love, Max xxxx

He read it over, and satisfied, he folded it neatly and placed it in
the small black velvet box.

Fleur came up from the spa with the relaxed look Max had hoped
for. "That was so great, Max. The therapist said it was a famous
Ayurvedic technique. They had hot oil dripping on my head and face.
It was amazing. Are you going to have one?"

"No. Not this time around. But I am looking forward to getting
my regular Balinese massages pretty soon. I miss feeling nurtured like
that. I'm going down to the lobby to see what looks good for us."

"Cool. I'm going to lie down for a little while. Come get me
whenever you're ready."

"You got it, kiddo. See you in a few."

Max thumbed through the lobby brochures regarding day trips
and places to check out in town. It was all new, so it didn't matter to
him. He was starting to feel that urge to get home. It was always funny
to him that even on a great vacation, when the time is almost up, his
mind would shift from where he was to where he would be going in
just a few more days.

Max knocked on their room door, then placed his key against
the electronic entry spot. He walked in to find his dear friend sound
asleep with the lights out. So, he opted for a hot bath.

The bathroom was nice. Not exceptional like the Leela Palaces,
but they did have assorted bath crystals and soaps. He chose the
lavender for relaxation, poured it under the hot running water, and

stepped into the big soaking tub. It was heaven. He let his head relax against a bath pillow while the water filled up just past his chest. The hot water and crystals worked their magic. By the time he stepped out of the tub, his legs were like rubber.

Fleur was sitting up against the pillows on her bed when Max came out of the bathroom. He'd requested two queen beds instead of a king. It made sense and he was sure Fleur would appreciate it. It was easy enough to get into bed together if that's what they wanted. This way, they each had their own space and their body language would take care of the rest.

Fleur was naked under the sheets. She sat up to show off her new necklace. "Max. This is so beautiful. Does it look good on me?"

Max moved over to sit on the edge of her bed. "A torn cloth from a second-hand store would look good on you, Fleur. I'm so happy you like it. You changed my life in so many ways. Some ways you aren't even aware of that are personal to me, but had such an impact. I love you, you little rascal. *Je t'aime de tout mon coeur.*"

Fleur put her arms around his shoulders to lean in and kiss him. "And I love you. So… what are we doing?"

"Well, I thought we could just take the hotel shuttle into town, walk around, shop a little, have a great dinner, then enjoy the mountain view. Tomorrow is our train ride. Is that okay? I know it's not all that exciting, but honestly, I'm a little tired and I've been thinking about going home and at Om Ham."

"It's the prefect plan. I feel the same. I want to get back to Bali, talk to Ali, and then figure out whether I'm headed to Paris or Los Angeles."

That was his perfect cue. He reached into his backpack to pull out one more surprise. He handed Fleur an envelope with something inside. "Here. I wasn't sure how you would take this, but I was trusting my instincts."

Fleur took the envelope from him with a curious smile. She pulled out a ticket, reading what it said aloud, "Bali to Paris with return."

"I hope I was not being presumptuous. I got you a ticket to Paris for a week from now. You can exchange it or use it, whatever you want. You can enjoy some Om Ham time, talk to Ali, and just let it all hang out. Do what makes you happy."

Fleur was crying as he spoke. "You are so amazing!" she said through her tears.

"You better stop crying. That's what got us into trouble in the first place."

Fleur laughed and hugged the favorite man in her life — other than her father, of course. Indeed, that *was* how it all began. Her credit card was ruined and she was crying at the reception desk at the same hostel Max was at over two years ago in Kintamani. He rescued her then by wiping her tears with laughter, paying for her room and being the best friend she could have ever wished for.

That night in Kintamani they slept together for the first time. This night, their last night in India, they slept in their own beds, enjoying the deepest sleep either had in a long while. They were like two best friends on a sleep over.

CHAPTER THIRTY-ONE

The Toy Train

The scene at the Kalka-Shimla Railway station was unimaginable, indescribable in a specific kind of way other than to say you had to see it to believe it. There were backpackers from all over the world there to take part in the experience of riding the train between the two cities.

The Toy Train is known worldwide for having the steepest climb of any train in India — 96 kilometers. The journey takes passengers through 100 tunnels during the journey between the two cities. The longest tunnel is almost a mile long. It goes from being really hot at Kalka to really cold up in the mountains of Shimla.

The train doors opened signaling a mad rush to get inside. The conductor stood on a platform to witness the sight he has seen and loved for many years. It was an experience of a lifetime that would never be forgotten.

Max and Fleur found a great spot with a bench seat they could both sit on. It faced forward, which is what they hoped for. When the whistle blew, they held hands and looked out the window. The train chugged its way out of the station to begin its slow descent winding down the ridge of the mountains to Kalka.

They were quiet. Fleur rested her head on Max's shoulder. She was full of questions, but in a good way. She felt everything would be great, no matter what she decided. She would let her heart take care of that.

As the train approached the first tunnel, young backpackers leaned halfway out the windows for a better view, like they were sticking their heads out of the sunroof of their car back home. The views were incredible to see. Unforgettable. The mountains surrounded them in every direction.

Max and Fleur sat quietly, their journey almost over. Fleur looked up at her friend, partner … pick a name, it didn't matter. "Max. I love you so much." She intertwined her fingers with his, resting in his lap. " I was wondering…

Before she could finish, the train was in the tunnel. The only sound that could be heard was the echoing of the train's squeaky wheels against the old iron tracks.

CHAPTER THIRTY-TWO

Endings are Beginnings

Max and Fleur returned to Bali each with their own unique memories of a great trip. They each added a little more relationship wisdom to their life's story. Fleur was happy to reunite with Ali. They knew they would always be friends, sometimes lovers, and always be true to their best interests. After reluctantly returning the keys to the villa to Max and Lea, they shared a suite at Om Ham for their last few days in Bali.

Lea returned from her Perth trip with Ingrid feeling ready for the next chapter in her life with Max. She got the sense that India was good for him. Their relationship was mostly the same, but there were little changes in him that she loved. He lost the aloofness that was driving her crazy. She wasn't sure if they would be lifetime partners, but he returned with a level of appreciation for her that made her happy. So happy, that when he went for a massage with his dear friend Master Ketut at Om Ham, she used the time to get the villa ready for his fiftieth birthday party.

Max loved being at Om Ham. It was his home, his Om. However dizzy he might feel on a given day or at any time, walking the grassy gardens there was his grounding. Doing that always relaxed him, healed him, soothed his nerves, before anyone ever told him there was a thing called *grounding*.

He'd always had his own bit of spiritually inside him that didn't require names for things. He didn't care what it was called. He felt it when he was doing it. It didn't need the validation of a label.

A voice interrupted his walking meditation. "Max, is that you?"

He stopped in his tracks. One could have said, *dead* in his tracks, considering who it was. "Leslie?" Who else could it be? Long, curly blonde hair, half angel half child, a wistful smile … an instant knot in his stomach.

"Hi, Max."

He looked back at her. For a moment, he had that feeling one has when someone punches you in the stomach so hard it takes your breath away. Om Ham was supposed to be his sanctuary from moments like this. Sometimes the universe has its own way of operating.

"Leslie," he said again, and smiled. He couldn't help himself. Happiness can do that to a person. "Welcome to Om Ham. If you haven't heard, I double as the official greeter."

"Ha. Thank you. It's nice to see that big smile of yours. The few photos you sent me were always from here. It's even more beautiful in person."

"It sure is. I tell my friends back home the very same thing. So, what finally convinced you to visit Bali?"

"I've been taking yoga classes, of all things, and my teacher is an old friend of yours, Erica. We were talking movies because the strike was going on, and when I mentioned a few shows I had worked on, your name came up. Then she told me how she was the leading lady in your movie, *Three on a Match*. We ended up having tea and talking for a while. She told me about Om Ham, how healing and inspirational it is, and I wanted to check it out."

Max was surprised the knot in his stomach was much smaller than he would have expected. Eight years since seeing the person standing in front of you with the same unexplained issues you used to want answers to was a lot to be confronted with. *Guru where are you?*

"That's very cool. Hi," he said again with a soft smile. "I'm glad you decided to come. It's magical place." He took a deep breath in. He maintained his state of calm and he was happy with himself for actually feeling okay with what was happening. "How long are you staying?"

"I'm not sure. I have an appointment with Master Ketut soon. Would you like to have lunch after, if you're not doing anything?"

He took a long pause. "All right. I'll meet you in the Tulsi dining room. The kitchen prepares a special drink for guests after a session with the Master. Let go of everything. You're in for something very special."

Master Ketut saw him talking to Leslie. He was on his way to the therapy room and stopped to see his friend. Guru put his hand on Max's heart as he often did when he greeted him. "Hello, Max." He could sense the energy between him and Leslie from the other side of the garden. He was there for his friend, even if he wasn't aware of it at the moment.

"I'm so good. Thank you, Guru. This is my friend, Leslie, from a long time ago. She's your next appointment."

Master Ketut looked at Leslie. "Nice to meet you, Leslie. You're from California?"

"Yes, Los Angeles."

The guru had his hand on Max's shoulder. He wasn't shy and always spoke his mind. "Ahh. So, this was the relationship you would talk to me about. I can feel the years as well as the love and anguish you had for each other."

"It was interesting, Guru," Max said smiling. He smiled at Leslie as well. There were no ill feelings and he felt free to talk openly, especially with the guru right there. "But, in the end, it pushed me here and for that I am very grateful."

"You have learned a lot, Max. Keep your spirit right where it is with your big heart. It will never let you down." Then Master Ketut looked at Leslie with those commanding eyes of his. "Come. We start in ten minutes." With that, the guru walked off to the spa. Healing was his gift to all who found their way to him.

Leslie could feel the energy and calm emanating from her old friend. "It seems you're very close. It's so wonderful you found a place you love. You look so happy. You deserve it."

"Thank you, Leslie. I feel blessed every day to be here. This is home for me. We all deserve to be happy. I'm happy for you too. For all the love in your life."

"Thank you, Max. I didn't know what to expect if I saw you here. I can sense the happiness inside you."

"It didn't come easily," he replied. "Don't be late. Go enjoy your treatment. I'll see you after, if you feel like sharing."

Max walked away to the pool. He felt he handled this unexpected meeting without revealing that he was shaking on the inside. The pool would be a big help. That was the only drug available.

Guru said never complain. Never make excuses. But he felt at least entitled to a moment or two of monkey mind. Eight years is a long time to not see or talk to someone who once asked for your hand in marriage, only to have it pulled away when it was no longer needed.

Max thought to himself about the long journey life takes us on and the many twists and turns that come along with it. As his consciousness changed, he realized that the sadness he imposed on himself was all of his own making. The famous "blessing in disguise."

When he met Dori and they got married, he finally felt the kind of love he dreamed about. It helped him move past all the other trivialities in life that we can use to blame for our lack of things.

It's funny, however, that no matter what we intellectualize, we can't cover up our deepest hurts, the pain that we really need to identify and conquer and let go of, to forgive ourselves for. And just like that, another opportunity arrives.

Max had lost all track of time since he heard Leslie's voice. He understood time was an illusion anyway, but when eight years turns into a minute, it can play tricks on you. He walked toward the Tulsi room for this long-awaited *talk* or whatever it would be. He sat down on one of the two chairs under the poolside gazebo. It was a favorite place for people to sit before and after their sessions with Master Ketut.

When Leslie saw him sitting there, she approached with a big smile. He got up to greet her. "How was it?"

"I'm tingling and laughing and crying. It was the most incredible body work therapy session I ever had."

"I'm happy for you, Leslie. It's cool you got to experience a little of what my life is like. People come from all over the world to see him and not everyone gets the opportunity you just had."

"I'm very thankful, Max. May I hug you?" Leslie didn't wait for an answer. She came up close to him and wrapped both arms around him as tight as she could. She just held her arms in place, pulling him close, rubbing up and down his back with long, loving strokes.

He didn't resist. He felt something from Leslie he never felt before. It was love. He felt it rushing through him, creating butterflies in his stomach.

Leslie stepped back a foot or two. "Max, please forgive me. You were always so kind to me, so loving. I see the man you have become, yet to me, you were always this man. I just didn't see it or acknowledge it. I am so truly sorry. I did love you and I do love you."

He took her hands in his, one over the other. "I love you, Leslie. I wish you the most amazing life to be filled with love. I learned I was the one who created all my own pain. You did nothing to me. You helped me find who I am in many ways. Most of all, I learned that I needed to love myself even more than I wanted someone else to love me. It's very healing and beautiful for you to say these words to me."

"I feel better too. I wish you all the best, Max, and for all the love you want to find you. You're a wonderful man and I'm sorry I never showed you how much I knew that all along. Have a sweet life."

"Stay here and enjoy the time you have. I'm so happy to see you here. Pretty crazy, huh?"

"It is pretty funny. I'm happy to see you here as well. Take care of yourself, Max. I love you."

"You too, Leslie. Take of yourself and keep enjoying life. I love you. I'm going to lie down in the garden." He knew as he walked away, that this was the last time he would see her — at least in this lifetime.

Leslie walked toward the pool. It was the best place to be after a session with Master Ketut. Max walked to the garden. Also, the best place to be after a session with the Master. Here at Om Ham, they are all the best places to be.

CHAPTER THIRTY-THREE

Home

L ea was in the villa with Ingrid, Ali, Fleur, Master Ketut and other guests from Om Ham. "HAPPY 50th B-DAY" banners hung near the front door and at the entrance to the garden near the French Doors in the master bedroom.

"Where's the birthday boy?" Fleur wanted to know.

"You know what? He could still be in the garden," Lea said. "Why don't you go get him? He set up this luxury tent with a nice futon mattress on a platform, speakers, and his own wifi hotspot so he could play his music and meditate outside. He even got screens made. His dream come true for fresh air without mosquitoes."

"Oh, my god. Can you imagine?" Fleur was not really that surprised. Max and his screen doors and windows. Fleur understood and could appreciate his desire for a mosquito-free environment. One bite is all it takes.

Fleur walked out to the tent. She unzipped the entry hatch and sat next to him on the bed. He was in a dream-like state. She had seen him many times after meditation, but this was different. He was almost floating off the bed.

"Wake up," she said, tapping his shoulder. His eyes opened but he had a very faraway look. His face was relaxed. There was an aura of peace all around him.

"Fleur?"

"Yes. Good guess. Are you having sex with any other French girls? Wake up. All your guests are here. Five minutes and Guru is bringing the cake out." She kissed his cheek and walked back towards the house.

He was in a different world for a minute. Somewhere between here and there. He squinted his eyes, rubbed them, then looked around his tent. His mind flooded with visions of the train, the ashram in Rishikesh, and most of all, making love to Fleur. It felt like a dream, but it was all so real. He raced out of the tent just in time to grab for Fleur's hand before she walked inside.

"Hey, wait for me." Fleur stopped and turned around. Max caught up, took her hand and pulled her close for a kiss. "Remember what you asked me on the train?" Fleur studied his face silently. "My answer is yes," he said.

"Happy Birthday!" The chorus rang out from the guests before Fleur could say anything. It was party time. Max walked in through the French doors, holding Fleur's hand. They would have to finish their conversation later.

Lea and Mobin, Guru, Ali and others clapped and smiled then sang a quick verse of happy birthday. Guru cut the cake and the guests got busy laughing, drinking and enjoying the day.

Max dashed into the bedroom to get the gift he had for Lea. It seemed like now was the perfect time. He called out, asking her to join him. She walked into their old master bedroom to find him standing at the open French doors. "What is it, Max? Everyone wants to be with you."

"I saw this in Delhi when I was out shopping, and I want you to have it."

She took the pouch from him, felt an object inside, then opened it to find the pendant and note. She looked at the alluring pendant totally taken by its beauty. The colors, the crystals, and the Ganesha figure inside made it look and feel magical. She read the note out loud: "Lea, I hope you will enjoy this Ganesha and me for a long time. Love, Max."

"Aww, Max. This is the sweetest gift ever. I will cherish it. I love you too. Come back inside. The guru has something for you."

"You go, I will be right there."

He had felt a soft breeze against his back while he was talking to Lea. When he turned toward the garden, he saw Satya in a long translucent peasant dress. "Satya? What are you doing here? What's going on?"

"You've had an amazing journey, my dear Max. You have traveled far and seen all of your life and met some amazing people. Go. Fleur is waiting for you. Your life is waiting for you. Love is waiting for you."

He walked through the open French doors, then stopped. He turned around, but Satya was gone." Slightly above him in a foggy mist, she was smiling down at him.

THE END

www.ingramcontent.com/pod-product-compliance
Lightning Source LLC
Chambersburg PA
CBHW060448310726

48977CB00001B/356